THE GETAWAY GROOM

Ginny Baird

THE GETAWAY GROOM
Published by
Winter Wedding Press

Copyright 2014
Ginny Baird
Trade Paperback
ISBN 978-1-942058-00-7

Edited by Linda Ingmanson
Cover by Dar Albert

About the Author

From the time that she could talk, romance author Ginny Baird was making up stories, much to the delight -- and consternation -- of her family and friends. By grade school, she'd turned that inclination into a talent, whereby her teacher allowed her to write and produce plays, rather than write boring book reports. Ginny continued writing throughout college, where she contributed articles to her literary campus weekly, then later pursued a career managing international projects with the US State Department.

Ginny's held an assortment of jobs, including school teacher, freelance fashion model, and greeting card writer, and has published more than twenty works of fiction and optioned ten screenplays. She's additionally published short stories, nonfiction and poetry, and admits to being a true romantic at heart.

Ginny is the author of several bestselling romantic comedies, including novellas in her *Holiday Brides Series*. She's a member of Romance Writers of America (RWA), the RWA Published Authors Network (PAN), and the RWA Published Authors Special Interest Chapter (PASIC).

When she's not writing, Ginny enjoys cooking, biking and spending time with her family in Tidewater, Virginia. She loves hearing from her readers by email at GinnyBairdRomance@gmail.com and welcome visitors to her website at http://www.ginnybairdromance.com.

Books by Ginny Baird

Holiday Brides Series
The Christmas Catch
The Holiday Bride
Mistletoe in Maine
Beach Blanket Santa
Baby, Be Mine

Summer Grooms Series
Must-Have Husband
My Lucky Groom
The Wedding Wish
The Getaway Groom

A Haunted Holidays Special Edition
The Ghost Next Door
(A Love Story)

Other Titles
Real Romance
The Sometime Bride
Santa Fe Fortune
How to Marry a Matador
Counterfeit Cowboy

Bundles
Real Romance and The Sometime Bride
(Gemini Edition)
Santa Fe Fortune and How to Marry a Matador
(Gemini Edition)
The Holiday Brides Collection
(Books 1—4)
A Summer Grooms Selection
(Books 1—3)
Wedding Bells Bundle

Short Stories
The Right Medicine
(Short Story & Novel Sampler)
Special Delivery
(A Valentine's Short Story)

Ginny Baird's

THE GETAWAY GROOM

Love on the run...

Chapter One

Mark Delacroix stood before the small chapel mirror and adjusted the blue bow tie that matched his eyes. The bridesmaid dresses were blue too. That had been Sandra's idea. Mark figured it was a small sacrifice to make. That, plus trimming his charcoal hair extra short. And, oh yeah, eliminating his typical three-day stubble.

His buddy Wayne patted his shoulder and smiled at their reflections. "You almost look presentable."

Mark raised his brow at his friend. "Scary, isn't it?"

"Petrifying."

Mark wondered if he was just having cold feet, or if something else was going on. This was supposed to be a great day. A spectacular event he was looking forward to. Though the church was small, the wedding was lavish. Sandra'd told him many times her dad had spent in the six figures on this bash. Mark almost wished she hadn't shared those numbers. It made him feel, he didn't know… *Beholden.*

"Look at it this way," Wayne said. "By this time tomorrow, it will be over."

"That's what I'm worried about."

Only his best man Wayne had the privilege of being in here. The other four groomsmen—all of them Sandra's brothers—were waiting outside.

Wayne's lips locked in a frown. "You're not having second thoughts?"

Mark shrugged.

"Everybody's got to get married sometime, right?"

"No." Wayne met his gaze. "Listen, man, it's not too late to stop it. The fat lady hasn't sung yet."

Just then they heard a woman's voice rising in a high soprano. The song was "Ave Maria." The ceremony had started. Mark swallowed hard.

He could do this, sure he could. Hadn't Sandra said that the time was right, and neither of them was getting any younger? It was true they were both in their early thirties, and each had said they wanted to have children. Of course, when they'd had that conversation, they'd been talking in general.

By now, Sandra had planned the whole thing out. Where their kids would attend prep school, how the family would summer in the Hamptons, which Ivy League each of their offspring should shoot for… And there wasn't even a baby yet!

Someone knocked on the door, and Wayne went to answer it. "Buddy," he told Mark. "It's time."

Wayne pulled back the door and stepped aside with surprise. It wasn't one of the groomsmen as expected. It was Sandra! She was dressed all in white in her designer gown, a thin veil flipped back over her head. "Ave Maria" was already on its second chorus.

"Isn't this bad luck?" Wayne asked.

"Can I have a minute with Mark?" Her eyes were all big and goopy like she was going to break down crying. They were blue like her mom's, and her wavy blonde hair was piled up under her veil.

"A minute's about all you've got," Wayne said, checking his cell. Then he exited and left them alone.

"Sandra?" Mark asked. "What's going on?"

She scuttled over to him, her crinoline crunching. "I couldn't…go through with it, not without—"

"You're calling off the wedding?"

"No." She sniffed into the hanky in her hand. It was something that had belonged to her grandmother. Something borrowed. It was old too. She'd hinted that the *something blue* was buried beneath her dress, and that Mark would get to see it later. "But, I do have something to tell you."

Mark was aware of a deafening silence. "Ave Maria" had stopped, and only a small dressing room clock ticked in the background.

"It's about Frank."

"Frank?" This hit Mark out of left field. Frank was some older guy Sandra worked with. He wasn't exactly her supervisor, but he did run the department Sandra wanted to become a part of. "What about him?"

Sandra brought the hanky to her mouth to muffle her cry. "I slept with him!"

"*What?*"

Someone rapped at the door. "Daughter, are you in there?"

Mark felt like someone had punched him in the gut, extra hard. "When?"

She blinked, dabbing her eyes. "You want a list of dates?"

"There was more than one?" Mark asked, aghast.

Her dad knocked again.

"Just a minute, Daddy!"

"We've got a whole church full waiting," he returned gruffly.

Mark ran a hand through his hair, sorry now he'd cut it. Sorry now he'd done anything Sandra had asked him to do. She'd been cheating on him. Cheating! "He's out there, isn't he?" Mark asked.

"His wife came too."

"Like that makes it so much better."

"Listen, Mark. I'm telling you this because I want to be fair. I want us to begin our marriage on a clean slate."

"You've got to be kidding me."

"No! I told Frank. Told him last night. It's over."

Mark's head reeled in disbelief. "You spoke to him after the rehearsal dinner?"

"During. He was there. Remember?"

Sure he was. *With his wife!* Alarm bells started ringing in Mark's head. Then his whole world went up in smoke. He could barely see through the fog to meet her expectant eyes.

"There." She heaved a little breath. "Now that it's done, I feel much better." Incredibly, her mouth turned up in a smile. "Baby, don't be mad."

Mark wasn't mad, he was suffocating. It was as if someone had gripped him by the throat and wouldn't let go. And they were choking the life out of him.

"Open the door," he told her urgently.

"You're right," she said sweetly. "We're already late."

Mark peered out into the narthex, where Wayne was waiting. Sandra's dad and her brothers stood by impatiently too. He spied a sea of blue beyond them and took that to be a gaggle of bridesmaids. But everything was spiraling in a fuzzy blur. Wayne met his gaze, his eyes widening. Somehow he understood that something had gone desperately wrong.

Sandra's dad took her by the elbow, giving her a sunny smile. "You look lovely." He led her toward the door to the sanctuary, and the bridesmaids all fell in line. He addressed Mark and Wayne and his sons. "You boys better get around up front."

They were supposed to enter near the altar, each taking his assigned place. Wayne held open the door, and the groomsmen began filing outside. When Mark slipped past him, Wayne caught him by the sleeve. "What's going on?"

Mark saw a bright flash of light before him, then a whole nursery of babies. All boys like Sandra's brothers. And they looked like Frank! He met Wayne's eyes. "I can't do this." He didn't need to explain what had happened. Wayne had his back.

"Then run, man. Make a break for it. *Now.*"

Mark's eyes flitted to the front of the church, where the groomsmen were headed. Then back to the sidewalk flanking the road. They were in an older part of town with historic houses, iconic buildings, and small eateries all clumped together. It was Saturday morning just before ten, so the foot traffic was light. If he took off now, he might get three blocks away before anyone noticed.

Mark's head swam, but there was a fire in his gut. *And this fire's going to consume me if I stand here another second.*

Wayne set his jaw and nodded. "*Just do it.*"

Mark glanced back in the church and saw Sandra's and her dad's eyes on him through the open door. Up ahead, her brothers had stopped and pivoted his way.

Mark sucked in a breath and gathered his nerve before sprinting in the opposite direction. His heels clicked against the sidewalk, dress shoes pinching as he went. But that didn't slow him down. Mark glanced over his shoulder to see Sandra's brothers shouting after him, following in hot pursuit as Sandra's dad bolted from the church. Wayne brought up the rear, hightailing it as fast as he could. *Holy cow,* Mark thought, racing forward. Then, he swung his arms into action and picked up his pace.

Chapter Two

Ivy Green carefully scooped the froth from the milk steamer into the cappuccino cup. Old man Winters was waiting on his morning fix. "Coming right up, Walt!" she called with a pleasant smile, carrying the cup over. Walt Winters had been coming to the Coffee Connection every day for the past two years and eight months. Nobody knew why he'd suddenly opted to make this a part of his daily routine. He'd started Ivy's third week here and was always waiting outside when she came to open up the shop.

She placed the cup on his table, and he lowered the newspaper he regularly bought from the box outside. His beard and mustache were white to match his hair, but they were neatly trimmed. "When you going to get yourself a boyfriend?" Walt's eyes were as dark as coffee beans. It had occurred to Ivy more than once that he must have been a handsome man in his prime.

She smiled and set down the two packs of natural brown sugar he always took in his coffee. "As soon as the right guy comes along." *And doesn't run out on me,* Ivy thought to herself but didn't say. She noticed movement behind him and stared out the shop's front window, spying a guy in a tuxedo racing by. *Weird.* Wait! There went another one… No, another three! And a middle-aged man! Finally, another young guy brought up the rear, shouting after them.

Walt turned to watch as well. "Some kind of contest going on?"

"I don't know." Ivy glanced around the small space, which stood empty. Walt was always the first one here, and no one else had arrived. "I don't know what that was, truthfully."

Walt rattled his paper and grumbled, "Looked suspiciously like a groom under the gun."

"What?"

"A runaway. You know, the type that skedaddles."

Yeah, Ivy knew that type *exactly*. "I'll get your water," she offered, walking back to the counter.

Since it was only her and Walt, she left the counter flip-top up while she went to work filling a plastic cup with ice. But the ice dispenser acted up again, spitting a pile of cubes onto the floor. *Great*. Ivy groaned. Now she'd have to mop that up before Eustis arrived. Eustis was her boss and very particular.

A blast of warm air blew toward her, and Ivy looked up, seeing a man had bolted in the door. He was about thirty with coal-black hair and a chiseled chin. His deep blue eyes were panicked. She suddenly realized it was the guy in the tuxedo, the one who'd been leading the parade of men.

"Please!" he said, breathing heavily. "You've got to…" His gaze darted to the front window, where the group of others tore by. Before Ivy knew it, he was with her behind the bar.

"You can't be back here!" she screeched.

Walt leapt to his feet. "Young man!" But before he could respond, the guy began skidding on melted ice.

"Arghh!" he cried as his dress shoes plowed through puddles, then started sliding. He went down hard with a *thud*, landing flat on his back, arms outstretched.

Ivy stared in horror at the terribly hot guy in a tux. Even in those fancy clothes, he looked buff. She thought he was tall, at least taller than her by a good three or four inches.

The café door whooshed open again, and an agitated middle-aged man burst into the room. "Did he come in here?" He had a crazed look on his face, like he was ready to deliver a pounding. Ivy was strictly opposed to violence and certainly didn't want any occurring right in front of her.

"Who?" she asked, noting Walt was inching his way toward the bar.

"That rogue who was supposed to marry my daughter!"

Ivy peeked at the man pressing his palms together in a pleading motion. He sure didn't look like the set-the-date-then-ditch type. Then again, Ivy's judgment wasn't spot-on in that department.

"Missy, I asked you a question!" the father of the bride demanded.

Walt took a step toward him. "Hold it right there, fella"

Mark stared up at the dark-haired beauty, his heart pounding. He didn't know how he'd found himself in this position, but now his life was in her hands. If she turned him over to Sandra's dad, who knew what would be left of Mark afterward. Probably not much. He certainly couldn't fight back against an old man.

The woman flagged a palm toward the door and spoke softly. "I'd appreciate it if you didn't raise your voice in here."

Mark could hear Sandra's dad huff on the far side of the counter. "I apologize. It's just been a very… What I mean is, it's a simple question. Yes or no?"

The brunette set one hand on her hip and motioned around the room with the other. She wore jeans and a dark T-shirt that very nearly matched her hair. She had bangs and pulled the rest of her hair back in a ponytail, exposing smooth cheekbones. "What does it look like to you?"

"We haven't seen a thing," another voice said in corroboration. It was then that Mark remembered the guy sitting in the corner when he'd blown in.

A poof of wind ruffled some rags tied to the cabinet handles above him, and yet another voice called, "Dad! We think we saw him! He went that way!" It was Jeb, Mark realized. Sandra's oldest brother. Then, in a flash, there were more scurrying footfalls, and they were gone.

"Who says nothing happens in Rosemont?" the old dude asked.

Instead of responding, the woman stared down at Mark with chocolate-colored eyes. They were mesmerizing, unforgettable...captivating Mark in an uncanny way. His heart stilled, then skipped a beat as she held his gaze. She twisted her lips to study him an extra long moment. Her lips were a luscious raspberry red. When she parted them to speak, Mark wasn't sure what to expect. At the very least, he anticipated a scolding. In contrast, her tone was light. "Don't you think you'd better say who you are?"

Mark partially righted himself on his elbows and shot her a humble grin. "Mark Delacroix. Nice to—"

The bottom of her low-heeled boot met his chest and pressed him back down. One eyebrow arched dangerously as she loomed over him. "*Delacroix?*" She angled her chin toward the front and spoke to the older guy Mark guessed was still there. "Call back the F.O.B."

"F.O.B.?" the old guy asked.

"Father of the bride."

Mark sputtered from his pose on the ground. "Wait! Hang on…"

But she cut him off with a cold stare. "Seems we have a traitor in our midst."

"Traitor?" Mark croaked, trying to sit up again. She pinned him down—hard. Man, that girl was strong. Especially when she was angry. But why was she so incensed? "Listen, we appear to have gotten off on the wrong—" A boot heel dug in. "Argh! Foot!"

"What are you doing to him back there?" the old man wondered.

"Putting him in his place," the woman answered. "Someone's got to do it."

"But why?" Mark squeaked.

Suddenly the old guy was at the counter, his dark eyes staring down at Mark as well.

"It's not what you've done, but what you're trying to do." Her eyes were smoldering, fierce. "Single-handedly ruin this town."

The door swooshed open, and the brunette stared toward it with a gasp. "Austin?"

"Hi, Ivy. Nice to see you too," a husky voice returned. Mark froze in place, the boot still centered on his chest.

The color in her cheeks deepened. "What brings you to town?"

"Haven't you heard?" he asked, drawing nearer. "I'm getting married."

"Don't!" Ivy warned.

"Don't what?"

"Take a step closer. I've just mopped the floor!"

"It doesn't look wet."

The older guy turned toward him. "It's one of those new-fangled cleaning products. Insta-dry. Though you can never be sure."

Mark had no clue what was going on but decided to play it safe by staying extra still. Maybe Ivy would get so distracted she'd forget all about him. Then he could stealthily slip out from under her boot and sneak away.

"Fine," Austin said. "I can tell you want to get rid of me. Not that I'd been planning to stay."

"Then why are you here?" the old man asked.

"To invite you to my wedding."

"Me? But I don't even know you."

"Not you. *Her.*"

He must have stared straight at Ivy, because she seemed to be holding her breath. "That's good of you," she said with a smirk.

"Not that I'd really expect you'd come. It was Caroline's idea."

"Caroline?"

"My fiancée."

"I see."

"Of course, Caroline said it would be hard on you. We'll understand if—"

"Hard?" Ivy cut in. "I hardly think so."

"You'll come, then?" Austin sputtered.

"My signif and I wouldn't miss it for the world."

"What the heck is a *signif*?" Austin demanded.

"Significant other," Ivy said primly. "That is, if you're sure it won't bother *you* seeing me with him?"

"I didn't know you were dating anybody."

Ivy gingerly lifted her boot off Mark's chest and glanced down.

"It hasn't really been your business to know, now has it?"

"No, but—"

"Why don't you just run along? I've got things to do here, and we're opening in ten minutes."

"Well, I sure didn't know you were seeing anyone," Austin grumbled. "This will be news to Caroline too."

"Likely make her happy," the old man quipped.

"Yes," Ivy added. "We'd hate for the bride to be jealous on her wedding day."

"Jealous?" Austin asked, befuddled.

"Didn't Ivy ask you to leave?" the old man questioned.

"Yeah, sure. I'm going," Austin said, making his retreat.

The old guy glanced at Ivy and whispered, "Got yourself into a pickle now."

Mark was just sitting up when the door whooshed open again, and a woman's high heels clickety-clacked across the room. What was this place? Grand Central Station? Before he could stand, a new person was peering down at him. She had springy red curls and a creamy complexion, with fine wrinkles surrounding her eyes. She stood beside the old man and shrieked.

"Heavens to Betsy! What have we here?"

"Mark Delacroix," Ivy reported.

"Is that a fact?"

"Ran out on his bride," the old man informed her.

"Well, well…" The redhead clucked her tongue and surveyed the damage. Mark noted for the first time he'd pulled over a napkin holder, a cup of ice, and a whole gallon of nonfat milk during his fall. The space around him was a disaster. "Aren't you good at making a mess of things?"

To Mark's surprise, his buddy Wayne peered over her shoulder. "There you are!" He glanced at the brunette, then down at the littered floor. "Did you do all that?"

Mark peeled himself off the floor, his tuxedo jacket sticking. He yanked it free, and it dripped with milk when he stood.

"Wow," Wayne said.

"I hope you're going to clean that up," the redhead added.

The next thing Mark knew, the *helpful* brunette was handing him a dustpan and broom. "I don't believe I've had the pleasure," he said smartly.

Her chocolate gaze met his. "The name is Ivy Green. But the pleasure's not mine."

While everyone in Rosemont had heard of Mark Delacroix, very few had met him. He'd swooped in under the cloak of night and bought out Chicken Fried Foods before anyone could say *snap*. Chicken Fried Foods was the mega packaging plant that employed most of the townsfolk. Now a swanky new beer-bottling place was going in, with tasting rooms and focus-group consultants from New York.

Had any thought been given to the hundreds of people who'd be put out of their jobs? No. Were there any plans to retrain them to work in the new business? No, again. Outsiders were being brought in from the north. Folks who yearned for a quieter way of life and clean country air for their children. What about the parents and kids who were already here? Ivy's cousin Grace was on the staff of the local paper and had covered the whole disgusting story. The details of the deal that had gone public, anyway. It was astounding a man like Mark could even have friends. He apparently had one, because the other guy was helping him now, bending low to retrieve a wad of soppy paper towels.

"I think that about does it." Mark accepted the dripping towels from his friend and dropped them in a large wastebasket. "Don't tell me," he said with a hint of sarcasm Ivy didn't appreciate. "You want me to mop and shine too?" Why was he being cool to her? Wasn't *she* the offended party? In fact, all of Rosemont was offended. To top it all off, he'd made a wreck of her shop.

She snatched back the broom and dustpan as he handed them over. "That will do for now," she said, noting a few regulars stepping inside.

Ivy felt something warm grip her hand, then saw Mark had wrapped his fingers around hers where she held on to the broom. Ivy's pulse fluttered. "I am sorry, you know. Sorry for ruining your day."

"Well, you did pick up," Eustis said from behind them. "That's something."

Mark raised his brow and waited. His friend must have been hovering somewhere in the background too. But Ivy couldn't see him. She was too overwhelmed by Mark's sea-blue gaze. It swept over her like waves in the ocean catching her up in its swell. His hand tightened around hers. "Thank you, though. Thanks for not giving me away."

Heat crept up her chin and fanned across her cheeks. "I would say anytime, but…" He withdrew his grasp, and Ivy sucked in a breath. "I wouldn't mean it."

"Not that I blame you one bit. And, hey…" He glanced at her leg. "I'm sorry about that too. I'll pay for the cleaning." Ivy looked down, seeing for the first time her jeans had been splattered with milk and coffee.

"I do my own wash."

His friend glanced at him and motioned toward the street with his chin. "My car's not that far away. We should probably make a break for it."

"Aren't you even going to apologize?" Walt asked.

"But I already—"

"Not to Ivy," Walt said. "To your bride."

Chapter Three

Mark knew he'd have to confront Sandra eventually. Even if he saw himself as the injured party, he'd need to explain why he'd walked. Okay, so maybe he'd sprinted. But in the grand scheme, what was the point in splitting hairs? She'd basically been the one to call things off with her admission. The very idea that Mark would be okay with her infidelity was totally absurd. Even someone as obtuse as Sandra should have seen that.

Still, Mark understood he might have told her this in person rather than racing off. That would have been the mature thing to do, if he'd been feeling like half a grownup at the time. Instead, he'd felt cornered and betrayed. In the most abysmal way.

Mark couldn't believe she'd stage the whole show here just to make a farce of it. Marrying in Rosemont had been her idea. She'd said it would play well for the townsfolk. And what people thought in a small town mattered. They did plan to settle here, after all. Or at least Mark was going to settle here initially. Sandra hadn't been sure she could make the transition. So she'd opted to keep her job in financial securities and commute to Rosemont on weekends.

Wayne pulled into the drive of the white stucco cottage that sat in a sunny field. It had a white picket fence and a smattering of colorful flowers strategically planted all around. They hadn't been sure Sandra would be here, but reasoned she would drop by at some point to gather her things. Not the least of which was the shiny little sports car she kept around back. She'd left it here when her maid of honor, Elizabeth, had driven her to the church.

"What are you going to say?" Wayne asked Mark.

"I'll try to keep it civil."

"And brief," Wayne suggested. "Don't let her pull you into something long-winded. You know where that always leads."

Yeah, Mark knew all right. He'd wind up in bed with her, as he had time and time again. Sandra had a sneaky way about her that got to his hormones. What with those big blue eyes, and that put-together figure, she could turn the head of any guy. And when she planted her mouth on his and pressed him back up against a wall, Mark could barely think straight. He liked to tell himself they had more than chemistry in common. They'd been building a connection based on mutual interests and goals. Now he saw that was all bull. While his ex-fiancée had been floating his boat, she'd been serving another captain too. Maybe more than one of them!

"What's that?" Wayne asked, alerting Mark's view to a couple of vehicles parked around the side of the house. Mark recognized the candy-apple-red coupe at once. But who was driving the luxury sedan with the out-of-state plates parked beside Mark's SUV?

"Maybe it's… Wait," Mark said, stopping himself. "Elizabeth doesn't drive that kind of car."

"No one in Sandra's family does either," Wayne observed.

Mark had an unsettling feeling about this. Way unsettling.

Wayne laid a hand on his tuxedo sleeve. "Want me to go in with you?"

"I'll handle it," Mark said, heading for the house.

Mark stepped onto the porch, spying movement through the sheer curtains draping the window. Behind him, Wayne still idled in his car. Mark spun in his direction, waving him away, and Wayne slowly drove off. A little too slowly, in Mark's opinion. What did Wayne believe? That Mark couldn't take care of things on his own? All he had to do was go in there like a civilized man and ask Sandra to pack her bags, if she hadn't already. His name was on the lease, not hers.

Mark laid his hand on the front doorknob but found it locked. He fished in his pocket for the keys, spying motion inside again. Mark leaned toward the window and peered through the gauzy white mist that cloaked his view. No way! But it was. Sandra was on the sofa— *beneath Frank*—with her wedding dress hiked up! Frank appeared to be nibbling a trail from her thigh down to her ankle.

Mark unlocked the door and burst through it.

"Mark!" Sandra shouted, her face beet red. Frank yanked something off her shoe with his teeth and shot to his feet. Was that Sandra's blue garter dangling from his mouth? "What are you doing home?" She quickly righted herself on the sofa, rearranging fluffy crinoline to cover her legs.

Mark's jaw dropped in disbelief. *In my house? On my sofa?* "I live here!" he returned furiously. "What's your excuse?" He stormed toward them, and Frank recoiled, shielding himself with his hands.

"Please!" he begged in a squirrelly tone. "Don't hit me!"

Mark gazed from his quivering double chin to his wing-tipped shoes, then back up into pale gray eyes. "Don't worry yourself."

Frank made a lame attempt to shield Sandra by stepping in front of her. "Or...or...her," he stammered, his temples bulging.

Mark blew out a breath and stroked his chin. He'd never imagine this day could go from bad to worse but it had. In fact, it had far surpassed that and had hit rock bottom. He slowly turned his eyes on Frank. "Do you mind?"

Without further encouragement, Frank moved out of the way. Sandra sat pertly on the sofa, adjusting some pins in her hair. To Mark's astonishment, he saw she still wore her wedding veil. She unabashedly met his gaze.

"You might have knocked."

"You might *have not*," Mark told her. "Not have done any of that! Not at the office!" He glared at Frank, who backed away. "Not in my house! For crying out loud, Sandra! What were you thinking? Or do you even think at all!"

"Now that was a little uncalled for," Frank offered. Mark wheeled on him, and Frank's Adam's apple rose and fell.

"Don't make me change my mind," Mark warned.

Frank crossed his arms. "Maybe," he said weakly. "Maybe I should leave the two of you alone to work this out?"

"Good thought," Mark agreed.

Frank glanced at Sandra.

"It's all right," she told him coolly. "I'll deal with Mark."

Awesome. Now I'm something to "deal with"? Well, let's see how Sandra deals with this. "You know," Mark said when the door closed at his back. "The funny thing is I was actually looking for you. Thinking to apologize."

Sandra feigned a pout. "And maybe you should. I never would have gone back to Frank if I hadn't been so devastated, you know." Big blue eyes welled with tears. "I mean… The way you ran out on me…" She choked back a sob. "Ran out on our wedding—"

"Sandra," Mark said, stopping her cold. "Save it for the priest. You'll probably need it."

"Huh?"

"During your next confession. If you ever go."

"Of course I'll go! We'll go together! There's so much we need to talk through." She scooted forward on the sofa, aiming to stand. "You and I, we…We have a future."

"No." Mark leaned forward and gently placed his hands on her shoulders, angling toward her. Her mouth quivered, ruby-red lipstick smudged outside its lines.

"You and I," he whispered hoarsely, "…*are done*."

She gasped, staring up at him.

Mark released her and dusted off his palms, swiping one against the other. "You have ten minutes to pack," he said, checking his cell. "The coffeemaker brews a full pot in twelve." Then he strode into the kitchen and ladled out some grounds. By the time the metallic beep signaled his java was ready, Mark heard tires squealing away down his gravel drive and peeling out onto the road.

Chapter Four

Two weeks later, Ivy set down her mug beside the newspaper article on the counter. If it hadn't been half-empty, coffee might have sloshed over its sides. Ivy couldn't believe the factory was closing. She'd known the change was coming, but not so quickly.

"It's true," Eustis said from beside her. "Myrtle Wilcox told me herself. Everybody got their pink slips this morning."

"That's horrible," Ivy protested. "Where will they go? What will they do?"

"I hear the auto parts factory is hiring over in Belleview," Walt informed them. He hovered over the news copy with a frown. "Not that this does folks any good who don't drive."

"No," Eustis agreed, "that's true."

Ivy shook her head and handed Walt back his paper. "Mark Delacroix wouldn't know a thing about walking to work. Probably owns a great big luxury vehicle, the hybrid kind."

Eustis patted Ivy's shoulder. "Well, darling. Best not to fret over spilt milk. Looks like the damage is done."

Ivy glanced down at the stain on her jeans that hadn't washed clean. Mark had made a mess of things all right. He couldn't just bulldoze into town and put people out on the street. What about her neighbor, Joy, the single mom who'd worked the evening shift while her sister watched the kids? And what about Joy's brother, Rob, who was working extra hours to save up for college tuition for his son? So many hopes and dreams were tied to Chicken Fried Foods. Mark had no idea.

Ivy dropped her rag to the counter, deciding someone ought to fill him in. She might not be able to stop what was happening, but perhaps she could slow it down. Or at least talk some sense into that big-city bachelor. He probably did this kind of thing all the time: ruin people's lives without thinking twice. Well, as long as Ivy was in Rosemont, Mark would have to think again. As the late mayor's daughter, Ivy took her civic responsibilities seriously. She cared about this town, and it had stood by her when times were tough. Rosemont had also warmly welcomed her back after her time away.

Ivy glanced around the sparsely occupied coffee shop. They never did much business on Monday. In fact, Eustis often toyed with making that their closing day. But being a preacher's widow and all, she saw fit to keep it shut on Sunday. Ivy turned to the older woman. "Can you hold down the fort a while?"

Eustis eyed her in an odd way. "Is something going on?"

Ivy untied her apron. "Yeah. A lot more than there should be."

Mark answered his door, stunned to see the pretty brunette from the café standing on his front porch. "Ivy?"

"Ivy Green, that's right." She appeared as attractive as he remembered, but her gaze was unwelcoming. Somehow Mark suspected this wasn't a social call. Suddenly, Mark remembered the offer he'd made. "You came about the cleaning?"

"Not exactly."

Why did she look so combative? As if she were prepared to take him on at any minute? Hand to fist? "Um, look... I'm not sure what this is about, but if it concerns the Coffee Connection, if I damaged something?"

"Do you have a minute?"

He held back the door, but her gaze flitted to the rockers on the porch instead. "I'd rather talk outside."

He shut the door behind him and motioned for her to sit. "Anything you'd like."

Ivy couldn't help but note how ragged Mark appeared. In the two weeks since she'd seen him, he'd grown a stubbly beard. Dark circles also ringed his eyes. If she didn't know better, Ivy would swear he hadn't slept in days. It was incredible he could still look hot in spite of that. But Ivy wasn't here to think about *hot*. She'd arrived on a very particular mission. "Mark..." She paused a beat. "May I call you that?"

"Of course."

"I'm not sure you know what you're doing."

"And I'm not sure I follow."

"I'm talking about Chicken Fried Foods and your shutting it down."

His face registered understanding. "I see."

"What do you see?"

"I get what this is. I'm the big, bad corporate guy from the outside. You're the champion for the underdog town? And you're here to set me straight?"

"Something like that."

"Nothing like that."

"What do you mean?"

"Look, Ivy." He gestured with his hand to the field across the way. Beyond it, mountains turned a purple haze in the sunlight. "Look around. What do you see?"

She puzzled at where he was going with this. "Garrett's farm. The Blue Ridge."

"It's stunning," he said. "Remarkable in its beauty."

"We're agreed." She turned her eyes on his. "So, why do you want to ruin it?"

"Ruin it? I aim to do nothing of the sort." His gaze was sincere. "Ivy, I want to help Rosemont. Help it stage a comeback."

"But Rosemont's doing fine." Even as she said it, there was a twinge of uncertainty in her stomach.

"Not if you read the latest census numbers and per capita reports."

The truth was other businesses *had* shut their doors, and that was well before this latest thing with Chicken Fried Foods. Upon her return to Rosemont after four years in school, Ivy had been stunned to note the number of empty storefronts on Main Street. Even more entities had folded in these last few years. And people were moving away, especially young people like her. She'd come back because she felt an obligation to Eustis and the town. But Ivy was aware not everyone her age felt that way. "You're saying that Rosemont's dying?"

His smile was tender, reassuring. "Not so much dying. More like ailing. "

"And you think you can make it better?"

"I believe I have a way to help, yes." His gaze lingered on Garrett's field, where a herd of cattle moseyed by. "Rosemont used to have a dairy, didn't it? And a meat-packing plant."

Ivy nodded in agreement. "Both of those."

"But times are changing, and small farms don't always stay in families."

Mark had obviously done his homework. Neither operation had stayed afloat, because when the older generation was ready to step down, their children had plans other than assuming those family businesses. Not that Ivy could blame them. She'd wanted a more independent, contemporary life for herself as well. That was why she'd gone off to school, but also why she returned. She'd decided she ought to apply her education by making her future in Rosemont. Rosemont was what she knew, and in a strange sense, she'd felt it needed her. The town had provided her with so much, especially in the way of support after her parents had died. Now, she wanted to give back. Maybe that, in part, was why she'd felt so strongly about talking to Mark.

"You're thinking a microbrewery can solve Rosemont's problems?"

"Not all of them, but it's a start. A start to revitalizing industry here, drawing in a new demographic."

"What about the old one?"

"It will be better for them too." He studied her a beat, and Ivy felt herself flush. "You're obviously a smart woman. Surely, you can see that anything that brings more business and tourists to town would be good for the economy at large."

"I don't know about *anything,*" she hedged, but Mark could tell the rationality of his argument was getting through. That was a good thing, considering the strain Mark had been under. If he could befriend at least one townsperson, that would be a start. It was tough to walk into a new place and constantly feel scrutinized. But Mark was good at his job and adept at winning people over, given enough time. Fortunately for him, he was a very patient guy.

"I promise it won't be as bad as you think. In fact, it will probably be a billion times better. Heck, you might even like the beer!"

"I don't drink," she deadpanned.

Mark wondered if he'd made some kind of gaff, until she cocked an eyebrow.

"Anything that comes in a fancy bottle."

Mark chuckled. "I'll ensure you only get served our best brew on tap."

"I don't know." She heaved a sigh, but her expression was softening. "Still don't know about any of this. What about the folks who have been put out of jobs?"

"I've given them all opportunities to come work for me."

Her eyes lit up. "What? But I thought I'd heard—"

"There won't be too many openings at the factory," he explained. "But there will be a gift shop attached, as well as a restaurant that serves barbeque across the street. I'll be accepting applications soon. Those who worked at Chicken Fried Foods will receive priority consideration."

Dark brown eyes met his. "Consideration? Or a guarantee?"

Mark's lips twitched in a grin. Ivy Green was one tough customer, but she also had a point. The people who'd worked at the factory were bound to be feeling insecure about their futures. Why just offer an opportunity when Mark could make a promise? He felt like a heel for not thinking of it himself. Maybe that was because this hadn't proved such a big problem in other places. The factory locations he'd previously transformed had been in larger metropolitan areas, so their workers hadn't been as dependent on one major employer. Rosemont was special because Rosemont was small. Three-thousand-people tiny.

"You're right," he conceded. "There won't be any question. If someone worked for Chicken Fried Foods, DelaStar Drafts will make a place for them."

Ivy sat there stunned, staring at Mark. She'd arrived primed to do battle with a beast. As it turned out, Mark was nothing like the ogre the *Rosemont Chronicle* had painted him to be. Ivy silently wondered if that was her cousin Grace's doing. Grace was forever sensationalizing things in order to sell more papers. Sort of like the time she'd reported old man Jacobs was the proud father of twins, with a promise to run the full story in the next day's edition. Since Jacobs was seventy-seven and had been widowed a number of years, folks had flocked to get the paper thinking he'd secretly married and kept a hidden bride. As it turned out, the "twins" were a pair of exotic parrots Jacob had ordered online. So when Grace reported "they arrived practically talking," that hadn't completely been a lie. Ivy sighed.

Mark studied her with concern. "I know it's getting warm. If you don't want to come in, maybe I can bring you some water?"

Ivy thanked him politely but declined, getting to her feet. "I really have to get going. I left Eustis alone at the Coffee Connection."

"Busy day, huh?"

"It will likely get busier," Ivy answered. She surveyed Mark as he stood there, his face bathed in sunlight that brought out the deep blue color of his eyes. He was nothing like she'd imagined him. Apart from the facts that he'd run out on his bride and trashed the Coffee Connection, Mark was actually shaping up to be a very nice guy. Ivy didn't know *why* he'd been a runaway groom, but in speaking with him now, it seemed there had to be a logical explanation. How could someone so committed to helping the town, turn around and be careless at heartbreak? The two things just didn't add up. And Ivy had always been good with math.

"I'm afraid this town's gotten the wrong impression about you."

"Wouldn't be the first time."

Ivy guessed that was true. People didn't often welcome strangers in their midst. Particularly strangers bent on making changes. "I'll see what I can do to set the record straight." She met his gaze. "Assuming you really meant what you said about guaranteeing work for those from Chicken Fried Foods."

"You have my gentleman's promise."

He shook Ivy's hand, and her pulse fluttered, just as it had when he'd wrapped his grasp around hers as she'd hung on to that silly broom. "I'm going to hold you to that."

His mouth turned up slightly higher on one side. "I work better under pressure."

Mark watched Ivy walk toward her car, thinking that Rosemont was an interesting place, already more interesting than Boston in some ways. There was something uniquely charming about the character of a small town. Mark had been here only a few weeks, and already he was making friends! Okay, so it was only one friend, and he wasn't exactly sure it would work out. But Mark hoped Ivy would be that. He'd rather have her in his corner than on the opposing side.

Mark recalled the ire in her eyes when she'd glared at him in her coffee shop. Whatever she'd thought of him then, her impression appeared to be improving. Mark was glad she'd stopped by. It had given him a chance to get to know her as well. Naturally, she'd been defensive when he'd first stormed into the Coffee Connection, particularly given the negative press he'd received. And he couldn't blame her for being on edge when her ex had unexpectedly dropped in with news of his impending nuptials. This hadn't just been a tough month for Mark, he realized. Ivy'd had her fair share of unpleasant surprises too.

Mark wondered about the history between Ivy and Austin. Clearly, it had been enough to do damage. Although Mark understood some things took a while to get past. Others could drag on for decades. Mark's lips turned down in a frown. Not that he'd give Sandra that sort of power over him. She'd invaded his life enough as it was. Two weeks of moping around and feeling sorry for himself was plenty. Now it was time to leave her behind. And that was just what Mark intended to do. Starting now. Today was the end of Mark's planned honeymoon break.

Tomorrow, he began work at the factory and would have a lot to keep him occupied. He had renovating and new construction to oversee. Not to mention a freshly made promise to fulfill. Mark was glad Ivy had taken him to task over ensuring work for Chicken Fried Foods' former employees. That was the right thing to do, and he knew it. *Not just a consideration but a guarantee.* Mark mused that there were few guarantees in life. His own existence hadn't granted him many. That didn't mean he couldn't pave a surer path for other folks out there. Forget leaving it up to the fates by placing ads online and in the paper. Every one of Chicken Fried Foods' former employees would be contacted in person and invited in to discuss a new job opportunity. Mark would talk to his project foreman in the morning and arrange it.

Chapter Five

Ivy blew into the Coffee Connection a bundle of nerves. Eustis sidled up beside her, refilling coffee. "So," the older woman asked, "how did everything go?"

Ivy glanced toward the door as Walt exited with a wave of his paper, then tied on her apron. "It went fine."

"Fine?" Eustis's brow rose, and Ivy felt her cheeks warm.

"I'll take table five," she said, indicating the two-top in the corner where a new couple had settled in.

Eustis laid a hand on her arm. "Like heck you will."

"What?"

Eustis locked on Ivy's gaze, then clucked her tongue. "I can't believe it. I mean, yeah, it's true I've seen him, so I can't fault you for being attracted—"

"I am *not* attracted to Mark Delacroix!" Ivy blurted out a little too loudly. She picked up some menus and cleared her throat. "What I mean is—"

"Sugar," Eustis said in a whisper, "just watch yourself, all right? That man is a snake. The slither-on-his-belly kind. You saw for yourself how he writhed right here on this floor."

Ivy nodded to the new customers, indicating she'd seen them and was coming. "Mark may not be as bad as everyone thinks." When she turned her back, Eustis gave a shrill whistle.

"Girl," she called after her, "don't you read the papers?"

Yes, she'd read every one. But nothing in those articles had prepared Ivy for meeting the real deal. When she'd surprised him at his house, he'd appeared almost reasonable. And, he seemed sincere in his desire to revitalize this town. Despite her outward protests to Eustis, Ivy couldn't help but admit she *was* a tiny bit attracted. Not in a schoolgirl-crush, head-over-heels way. In fact, not in a romantic way at all! It was more like observational. Ivy could appreciate Mark for being a confident, sexy man, but that didn't necessarily mean she wanted him for herself.

When she returned behind the counter with her order, Eustis snatched it from her with a frown. "So, did you do it? Accomplish what you set out to do?"

"I talked to him, yes."

"About Chicken Fried Foods?"

"He's guaranteeing all those workers jobs. One way or another, he'll find a place for each of them."

Eustis's jaw dropped. "How did you accomplish that?"

Ivy shrugged coyly. "I've got my ways."

Mark stood before the bathroom mirror, shaving his thickening stubble. *Just look at me! I should be ashamed of myself.* Sure, he'd taken a hit to the heart, but that was no excuse for letting the rest of him go to rot. He had a life to lead and a reputation to uphold... Mark stopped himself. No. He had a reputation to *build* in this town. And Ivy Green was going to help him. Mark had learned a lesson long ago. It didn't matter how much of the world was against you, as long as you had one friend in your corner, you could make it. His mom had told him that in the seventh grade after they'd relocated to a different town. Being the new boy in middle school had proved a hard transition for Mark. Since he'd moved north from the south, his accent was different from the rest of the kids, and in many ways, he didn't fit in.

Then he'd had a breakthrough. Another newcomer arrived from the Midwest, who'd sounded just as funny and out of place as Mark had to the others. Wayne and he played on the baseball team together, and became fast friends. By the time they'd graduated, both were among the most popular boys in school, with a large group of friends and promising futures ahead.

Mark splashed water on his face, then ran damp fingers through his hair, studying his reflection. *Now that looks like a guy prepared to run things,* he told himself with a grin. And he was going to run them right. While Mark often arrived in places under a dark cloud of suspicion, he'd left each operation walking in sunshine. Mark really did know how to turn ailing businesses around—and start new ones. He also saw what was good for a town. The people of Rosemont needed DelaStar Drafts just as badly as it needed them. Besides, this seemed a quiet enough, peaceful place. The right environment in which Mark could stage his retreat from women for the next little while.

"What?" he said into the mirror. "I never said I was attracted!"

Not that he could help noticing how pretty Ivy was, or the way her big brown eyes had centered on his when she'd been about to throttle him in the café. Or the way she'd packed that dynamite figure into a T-shirt and jeans. *Or* how she'd turned almost embarrassingly sweet as she'd backed toward her car, nearly tripping over her own feet.

Wow, Mark mused, his cheeks sagging, *this is worse than I thought!*

Then he splashed more water on his face, determined to salvage the rest of the day. That meant focusing on work and putting thoughts of one stunning brunette well out of mind. So what if he found her appealing? Any red-blooded guy in his right mind would feel the same. It was one thing to notice. Taking action was another matter entirely. And, given his track record, Mark understood he needed to keep any impulsive actions at bay.

Chapter Six

The following week, Walt met Ivy outside the Coffee Connection. A morning storm was upon them, rain driving down hard on the sidewalk and splattering up at Ivy as she wrestled to unlock the door. Walt lifted his golf-size umbrella to shield them both from the deluge, but that didn't keep Ivy's sneakers from getting soaked. She finally got the key to turn in the ornery lock and threw open the door.

Walt let her walk in first, then shook out his umbrella and stepped inside. "Suppose you've heard the news," he said, pulling the rolled-up paper from under his arm and flattening it out on a table. It was damp at either end.

Ivy took off her slicker and hung it up. "News?"

She turned on the lights and started setting up behind the counter.

"Right here in today's edition," he said, thumping the paper. "That Mark Delacroix is causing a stir."

Ivy paused in her work, holding a large pitcher of water she'd been about to pour into the coffee brewer. "What are you talking about, Walt?"

"J-O-B-S."

Ivy finished making the coffee, then looked up. "Yeah?"

"Seems he's giving them away like candy. Even your cousin Grace has something nice to say about him."

"Now, that *is* news," Ivy said with a laugh, knowing Grace rarely got a story straight. She hoped the talk she'd had with her had helped. All her previous pieces on Mark had been pretty unflattering. Now that

Ivy had seen Mark in person and had gotten to talk to him a little more, she couldn't believe he was a greedy monster. *He's more like a prince of progress*, Ivy thought, recalling his deep blue gaze.

Walt caught her off guard with a startled look. "Might want to watch what you're doing there."

Ivy stared at the coffeemaker that was spewing hot liquid. "Oh no!" She'd forgotten to insert the carafe! Ivy yelped, springing back and grabbed for some rags.

Walt rushed over to help with his newspaper, dumping it on the counter to catch the pools that were spreading. The front-page article lay on top, Mark's handsome mug quickly overcome by coffee.

"How did you guess I take mine black?"

Ivy glanced up to see Mark had appeared—in the flesh! She fumbled with the side of the machine, finding the switch and shutting it off. "Mark! How did you get in—"

He studied the mess on the floor, then met her eyes. "Walked through the door. Aren't you open for business?"

"Not yet," she rushed in. "I was just getting started."

"Need help with that?" he asked, indicating the mess.

"Thanks," she said, embarrassed, "but I think you've done enough cleaning up around here."

Just then, Eustis pushed through the door, bringing a swell of rain splatter with her. "Sweet cherry pie, what's all this?" Her eyes fell on Mark. "Again?"

He held up his hands, and Eustis glanced at Ivy, getting it. "Rough start to your day?" she asked Ivy, who was still mopping up.

"I've had better."

"I don't think you should decide yet."

Ivy met Mark's gaze through the short dark curtain of her bangs. His eyes were penetrating and every bit as blue as she remembered. "I think I'm plenty in a position to judge," she said, still kneeling. Just when Ivy was one hundred percent positive her morning couldn't get any worse, Austin walked in the door. Wait! It wasn't *just* Austin. It was Austin and some pretty blonde.

"Caroline," Austin said in his big booming voice, "*this* is the Coffee Connection, the place I've been telling you about." Ivy was *so* relieved she hadn't married him! She would have spent her life in earplugs!

The girl beamed up at him, then said as if reciting, "*Best peach pie in the south.*"

"It's cherry pie today," Eustis deadpanned.

Walt pointed to the chalkboard on the wall. "That's what's on the menu."

"That's all right, darling," Austin said, hugging Caroline close. "Plenty of other tasty treats to have with our coffee. Right?" he asked, eying Ivy.

She smirked, paper towels dripping. "No doubt you'll find something to your liking."

Austin's lips pulled into a thin, hard line. "No doubt."

The woman strode over on bouncy little steps, her short skirt highlighting the curves of her calves. "I don't believe we've been introduced," she said, holding out her hand. "I'm Caroline."

Ivy ditched the paper towels in the wastebasket and wiped her hands on her jeans. "Ivy," she said without accepting the gesture. "I would, but…" She shrugged.

Caroline's eyes darted to Ivy's soiled clothing, then back up to her face. "Ivy?" She glanced quickly at Austin. "You're not...?"

"Allow me to introduce myself," Mark said stepping forward. He took Austin's hand with a firm squeeze, then nodded at Caroline. "Mark Delacroix."

Austin's eyes lit with recognition. "You're that new guy we've been hearing about."

"I'll only own up to that if what you've been hearing has been good."

"I hear you're making changes."

"Good ones, I hope?" Caroline asked.

"Only the best!" Ivy surprised Mark by speaking brightly from the corner. She walked toward them, tying on a fresh apron. "Mark's in Rosemont to do some good."

Austin blew a doubtful breath. "That so?"

"Says right here in the—" Walt interceded. Then he glanced toward the trashcan, remembering.

Eustis twisted her lips and scrubbed down the counter. She was applying so much muscle, Mark feared she'd crack it. "The truth is," she said, directing her comment at Austin, "we're not open yet."

Caroline blinked. "But this place is packed!"

"She comes from an even smaller town," Austin explained.

"What's he doing here?" Caroline asked, indicating Walt.

"He owns the place," Eustis said without missing a beat. Mark had no idea whether that was true or not, but he suspected it wasn't.

Walt picked up a menu, studying it hard.

Austin angled his chin in Mark's direction but spoke to Ivy. "How about *him*?"

Mark hadn't quite liked the way he'd said that with a bone of contention in his voice. He didn't precisely care for Austin's stance either. Without meaning to, Mark mentally sized up Austin, figuring he could take him on if necessary. Yeah, the other man was broader across the chest and a little beefier in the middle, but Mark was strong from hauling kegs in a way no country boy could anticipate. He'd hate to have to prove that point. "I believe the lady said we're closed."

Eustis righted herself and viewed Mark with appreciation.

"*We,* now?" Austin's tone rose, mocking. "Are you one of the owners too?"

"No, he's someone more important," Ivy said harshly, as if nobody could mess with her. Caroline backed up a step, shielding herself behind Austin.

"Well, please," Austin said, his palms splayed open. "Enlighten us."

"Mark is... He's... Not that it's any of your business..." Ivy hesitated just a fraction of a second too long.

"It isn't," Mark said, joining Ivy at her side. "You can keep what's between us as private as you want to."

"Between you?" Austin asked, puzzled.

"Shut the door!" Caroline squealed with delight. "You two are an item?"

Austin's color paled as he stared at Ivy. "This guy is your *signif*?"

Caroline appeared thrilled. "How cute! You'll have to come to our wedding!"

Austin spoke, shell-shocked. "She's already invited."

"Who is?" Caroline asked, turning toward him. Then her gaze fell on Ivy, as Ivy's previous involvement with Austin dawned. "Oh!"

"Out with the old, in with the new!" Mark smiled brightly, pulling Ivy toward him in a one-armed hug. "Right, *baby*?" he said, giving her shoulder a tug.

Eustis dropped her jaw, and across the room, Walt motioned for her to shut it.

Ivy stood there tongue-tied, unable to believe what was happening. Was Mark defending her in front of Austin? And was he actually trying to help her save face by pretending to be her boyfriend? "Right," she stammered uncertainly. "That's absolutely correct!"

Austin narrowed his eyes. "That's some high-falutin' education you got at the costly university of yours."

"And that's an awfully big mouth you grew during your time out of town," Ivy heatedly contested.

Mark held her tighter. "It's all right, Ivy. You don't need to say any more."

"No, I guess you don't." Austin's gaze was cold. "You've already said it all."

Ivy studied him hopefully, then glanced at Caroline, forcing a disappointed frown. "So, I suppose I'm no longer invited to the wedding?"

Caroline nudged Austin, then whispered, "Sugar, that wouldn't be right. To disinvite somebody."

"I wouldn't think of it," Austin said firmly. Then he linked his arm in Caroline's, steering her toward the door. "We'll be expecting you both." He gave a tilt to his mouth that didn't appear friendly. "With bells on. And, oh, hey!" He turned to stare at Walt, then Eustis. "Y'all are invited too."

Chapter Seven

Eustis rapidly fanned herself with rag. "Heavens! I thought they'd come to fisticuffs in here!"

"I might have helped out," Walt said, standing.

"Sit back down, you old fool," Eustis answered. "Let me bring you your coffee."

Walt's lips twisted in a grin. "Why, Eustis, are you flirting with me?"

"Don't flatter yourself."

"Stopped that years ago."

"What do you mean?" Eustis asked him.

"Only that I'm old enough to know better."

"About…?"

"Supposing it's *all about me*."

Eustis eyed him appreciatively before proceeding. "Spoken like a wise man."

"I know a thing or two," he said without meeting her gaze again.

Eustis prepared his cappuccino and carried it over, with two packaged sugars. "Want anything else?"

"Got all I need with you around."

Eustis stood up a bit straighter while Ivy and Mark exchanged glances.

"I want to thank you," Ivy told Mark. "Thank you for what you said to Austin, though it totally wasn't necessary."

"Oh yes, it was," Eustis called from the corner.

Walt nodded in agreement, then winked at Eustis.

For the life of her, Ivy could have sworn Eustis blushed. Ivy didn't know what was making Walt so feisty this morning. She'd never seen him hit on Eustis before. In fact, she'd sort of suspected he was way beyond hitting on anybody. Just went to prove how deeply Ivy could be wrong.

"Listen…" Mark spoke in a whisper, turning his attention on Ivy. "I didn't mean for that to happen. The boyfriend thing. It just kind of—"

"Slipped out?" she guessed.

"Yeah, that."

"Look, Mark. It was very good of you to step in, but just because Austin is a great big bully, that doesn't mean you need to feel you—"

"He is, isn't he?" Mark observed. "Something of a bully, I mean."

Ivy shrugged. "I guess he still hasn't gotten over it."

"Gotten over what?"

Walt and Eustis exchanged knowing glances.

"You left him?" Mark asked.

Ivy blinked hard. She felt tears in her eyes but fought to contain them. She absolutely would *not* break down and start crying. When Austin left her at the altar, her whole world had caved in. But that was before Ivy understood that she held the power to change it. She'd gotten out of Rosemont to secure an education, then had returned here to prove to everyone that Ivy Green wasn't any sort of quitter. "It was the other way around."

Mark drew a breath, then spoke sincerely. "I'm sorry, Ivy."

She adjusted her ponytail and straightened her apron. "I'm over it."

Mark seemed to be wondering if she was.

A group of teenagers entered. They looked like kids from the local high school. Ivy motioned for them to have a seat. "I'll talk to you later," she told Mark, indicating she had work to do. But her tone was grateful.

"I'd like that."

"Me too."

He met her gaze, and Ivy's heart stilled.

"Might help if I have your number."

Mark shoved his hands in his pockets and headed down Main Street toward the factory. What sort of a guy walks out on a woman like Ivy? The type who can't appreciate what he's got, Mark decided. And he knew a thing or two about runaway grooms. In fact, he was an expert. He couldn't imagine someone like Ivy committing the sort of infraction Sandra had. No way. Mark stopped walking a moment to consider his snap judgment. He couldn't be sure how he knew Ivy well enough to surmise she wouldn't cheat on a guy, but everything in his gut told him she wouldn't.

Here was a woman who cared about people, her "peeps"—her town. She seemed genuine and sincere. Not like the type who would jerk somebody around. Of course, Mark hadn't thought that about Sandra either. Then again, those times were different. His radar hadn't been turned on. Now, it was finely tuned, and Ivy Green simply didn't seem the sort. In truth, she appeared more like him. Someone who knew what it was like to be on the receiving end of heartache, but who was tough enough to bounce back and get in that ring for another round.

Another round? Who on earth did Mark imagine Ivy might become interested in? Not him. And clearly, Mark couldn't become interested in her. He liked her, sure. And felt motivated to help. He'd met those Austin types before and didn't care for the lot of them. Helping

Ivy move beyond someone like that wouldn't just give Mark pleasure, he'd consider it his civic duty. Because sooner or later, the Austins of this world ultimately had to grasp that it wasn't right to treat others like dirt.

Mark laid a hand on the door to his building, then paused, questioning his motives. Was he really so intent on helping Ivy, or was this merely some veiled retribution aimed at his ex? He finally decided it didn't matter. The end game was the same. If nothing else, Mark could offer Ivy solidarity. He knew firsthand how it felt to be let down. He also understood how much it meant to have a friend stand in your corner.

Mark thought of Wayne, who'd always been there for him. Ivy probably had girlfriends she could count on, but not a man who could fill out a suit and stand by her side. Mark had run the numbers on Rosemont and knew that most single guys here were under the age of eighteen or over sixty. If Ivy had a boyfriend who was her real *signif*, she sure hadn't said so. This led Mark to believe she was on her own. And her going solo to Austin's wedding didn't seem like a stellar plan. Better for Mark and Ivy to go together. After all, the happy couple was already expecting them.

Ivy served the rest of the table, her hands trembling as she set down the final two coffee mugs. She couldn't believe she'd actually given Mark her number!

"Will there be anything else?" Ivy asked the group.

The kids were in for pastries and chatter, all eagerly discussing their plans for summer jobs. Some were still searching; others already had opportunities lined up. One was even working as an intern at the paper, assisting Ivy's cousin Grace with fact checking. Ivy conceded that was a much-needed post.

"No thanks," one of the guys said for the others. "Just our checks?"

"Oh, and…" a girl with layered blonde hair asked. "Can they be separate?"

Ivy nodded and returned to the counter, where Eustis was whistling.

"Why, Eustis Blair," she teased the other woman in a low whisper. "If I didn't know better, I'd swear that was a love song."

"Shut your mouth," Eustis snapped back. But it looked like she was suppressing a grin.

"I see that Walt's gone," Ivy said, checking the corner.

"Yeah, but he left a tip."

"He usually does," Ivy replied, not thinking much of it. Then Eustis showed her the simple café napkin upon which Walt had scrawled in ink pen, *Coffee sometime? Someplace else?*

Ivy grabbed Eustis's arm and whispered, "Walt asked you out?"

The older woman shrugged. "He left the note beside a small pile of bills."

"Big tipper."

Eustis turned to her. "A little ballsy, don't you think?"

Ivy set a hand on her hip and studied the attractive redhead. There was a hint of mischief in her eyes. "You're considering it, aren't you?" Ivy asked.

Eustis shrugged. "Mary's been gone for years," she said referring to Walt's late wife.

"At least ten," Ivy agreed. "I recall Mama going to the funeral when I was just a kid."

"The whole town went," Eustis remembered. "Everyone liked her."

"Nice woman, yeah."

"With a soft spot for pets."

"Whatever happened to all those cats she rescued?"

"I guess most of them stayed with Walt."

"He never talks about them."

"They'd have to be long gone by now."

"It must get lonely," Ivy said, "up in that big house on the hill."

"Probably why Walt spends his mornings here."

"That's what I used to think." Ivy giggled. "Until I suspected the truth."

Eustis's eyebrows shot up.

"That he's got a crush on the shop owner."

Eustis swatted her with a rag. "You think you know so much!"

"Don't I?" Ivy teased. "Love unrequited? How could I be wrong?"

Eustis turned her back and sashayed away, with an uncustomary sway to her hips. "Maybe the feeling's mutual."

Ivy was so surprised by her words that she burst into laughter.

Chapter Eight

Later that evening, Mark called Ivy.

"Hey," she said, attempting to infuse a coolness into her voice she in no way felt. Ivy had thought of nothing but Mark all afternoon. After a few minutes of chitchat, he broached the subject.

"You know, I was thinking," he said. "I never got the date of Austin's wedding."

"It's two weeks from Saturday. Why?"

"Good. That gives us time."

"For…?"

"To get to know each other a little better. Don't you think that's wise? I mean, we can't just walk in there like strangers and get everyone to believe—"

"Listen, Mark. What you did today was really sweet, and I totally appreciated it, but I don't want you to feel you have to—"

"What if I want to?"

Ivy caught her breath. "What?"

"I'm talking about taking you to Austin's wedding, Ivy—for all the right reasons. It will give you some breathing room and allow me to meet more folks in Rosemont. It could work out well for the two of us."

Ivy had to admit that getting *breathing room* sounded very appealing. If she had a date on her arm, she wouldn't have to deal with those "poor Ivy" looks the older women were constantly doling out when they saw her alone at social functions. Everyone knew she'd been ditched, just as they were equally aware Ivy hadn't seriously taken up with anyone since Austin. Ivy also didn't mind the notion of introducing Mark around. She'd already offered to help improve his reputation, and what better way than by giving people a chance to know him? The only catch was Ivy didn't believe they could pull off the couple charade.

"That's a really nice offer," she said, "but I don't think it will work. No one in Rosemont will believe you're my boyfriend. Austin was only fooled because he's been living away."

"You're right. I've thought about that."

"You have?"

"Sure. Folks have likely heard I recently ran out on a wedding. My own. It's also common knowledge you haven't dated since Austin. At least not seriously."

Ivy's heart thumped. She wondered how he'd pieced that together. Had someone been talking, or was Mark simply reading between the lines? "Well, I…" She stumbled through the words. "I hardly see how that matters."

"It matters because in everybody's eyes we're an unlikely pair."

That was certainly true, Ivy conceded. Who on earth would buy that Mark had come to town to marry one girl, then had suddenly hooked up with another?

"Which is why we're going to insist we're not involved."

"What?" Ivy asked, dropping the thread.

"In fact, we're going to heartily protest."

Ivy's head spun. "But you already told—"

"We'll say Austin and Caroline must have misheard. It was some simple mistake. Because, naturally, you and I barely know each other. We're just attending the wedding together as friends!"

"Friends."

"Precisely."

"And that will…?"

Mark lowered his voice in a conspiratorial fashion. "Make everybody believe the exact opposite. That we're desperately in love, but are covering up for appearances' sake."

It took only a fraction of a second for Ivy to realize he was right. That was just the sort of scandal Rosemont loved to sink its teeth into. Take two people who had no business being together, and plant the seed that they might be secretly involved. The more Ivy and Mark insisted it wasn't true, the more firmly everyone in the small town would believe they were an item, including Austin and Caroline.

"You really want to do this, don't you?" Ivy asked, amazed.

"I'm game if you are."

Ivy felt her lips tug into a grin so broad her cheeks hurt.

"*You,*" she said into her cell, "are a stark raving genius."

They decided to rendezvous two days later for lunch and strategizing. Since he set his own hours, it was easy for Mark to get time away from the factory, and Ivy wasn't working until that afternoon. They met at the new bistro Mark had opened across the street from DelaStar Drafts. The place offered deli sandwiches, barbeque, and a broad selection of beers. When Ivy walked in the door, Mark had already grabbed them a table. She turned toward him with a grin, and her smile lit up the whole room. Outside, thunder boomed and rain streamed down against the small tin roof. The building was a converted gas station, but just the right size for a cozy café, offering them shelter from the pounding rain. "I figured you wouldn't want to sit on the porch," Mark said when Ivy joined him.

"Maybe another time." She collapsed her umbrella, then laid it against the side of the booth. "I see you put a lot of tables out there."

"So people can get a view of the factory, yeah. We're working on replacing the windows. Making them floor-to-ceiling on this side. That will let in the light and also allow a view of the bottling operation from over here."

"So people can sit on the porch and sample, while watching how the beer is made?"

"Only the final phase, but for some, that part's the most exciting."

"Caps going onto the bottles?" Ivy asked with a laugh.

He held up a hand in correction. "Twist caps."

"Of course!"

"And environmentally friendly."

"How so?"

Two bottles of beer sat on their table and appeared to be ice-cold. Mark must have ordered these early to have them waiting. He offered one to Ivy.

"Better not," she said. "I'm working later."

"Me too. That's why I'm only having one." He shrugged, then shot her a grin. "Quality control." Mark twisted the cap off the bottle and flipped it over in his palm. The underside of the cap was stamped with a message: *Please recycle. 5 pts.*

"Five points?" Ivy wondered. "What's that?"

"People earn credits when they bring back the bottles."

"You mean like credits for more beer?"

"Nothing as mundane as that." He flagged over a waiter and offered Ivy something else to drink. She took iced tea.

"You were saying?" she asked when their server had left.

Mark pulled a pamphlet from his pocket and shared it with her. Ivy read the descriptions with interest. "Watershed protection… Wildlife preservation… The Nature Conservancy… Wow." She met his gaze. "You weren't kidding about environmentally friendly. Do you mean to say the factory contributes a portion of its profits to those places when patrons recycle?"

Mark nodded. "There's a scan code on every six-pack that buyers can use to access the information in this booklet online." He tucked the brochure back in his pocket. "And all credits go to benefit organizations in the local area. So when you bring back, you give back. And not just to DelaStar Drafts. Though it's good for us too, because we can reuse the bottles."

"That's really cool, Mark. How come you didn't share any of that with the papers?"

Blue eyes twinkled. "Grace didn't ask."

"Does this work all over the country, or only the areas surrounding your factories?"

"It's pretty localized right now, but we're hoping to take it global."

"As in worldwide?"

Mark grinned, and Ivy's pulsed fluttered. "That's the plan. Some day."

Ivy had never met anyone with such big plans. It almost blew her mind. "You're one ambitious man, Mark Delacroix."

"I like what I do. It makes people happy."

"As long as they drink responsibly," Ivy said, holding up her tea.

"I'm all for that." He handed her a menu. "Might want to take a look."

"Any recommendations?"

"The Montecristo's awfully good."

"Let's both have one."

He smiled in agreement, then ordered for the two of them. Ivy couldn't believe how easy Mark was to talk to. She never might have guessed it from their first introduction. Then again, they'd met under less than ideal circumstances.

"How about you?" he asked a short time later when their sandwiches arrived. "Got anything big in mind? Something you want to do?"

Ivy took a bite of her hot chicken and cheese sandwich and, my, it was delicious. "I'm still trying to figure that out."

"That's okay." His look was reassuring. "You've got time. What are you? Barely twenty-five?"

"Twenty-seven and a half. Thank you very much."

Mark chuckled. "I've got you by three-and-three-quarters years."

Her gaze widened. "You're thirty?"

"*Plus.*" He lowered his voice to a whisper. "Does that scare you?"

Ivy leaned forward and whispered back, "Should it?"

"Only if you're afraid of older men."

"You're not that much older," Ivy challenged. She set down her sandwich to dab her mouth with a napkin, then studied him up and down. "I'm actually impressed."

"Yeah?"

"That you've accomplished all you have by your age."

"I've worked hard."

"It shows."

Mark cocked his head to the side. "You're an interesting woman, Ivy Green."

"Oh?"

"The first time you met me, you didn't admire me at all. In fact, you were ready to throw me to the wolves."

"That's because I didn't know you."

"You still don't. Much."

"I know you a lot better than I did then."

"True." He polished off his sandwich, then pushed his plate aside. "But it seems the score's a little uneven. You know what I do and where I live, but…" He dove into her eyes, and Ivy felt herself flush. "I barely know a thing about you."

"You know where I work."

"And that you went with Austin."

"That too."

"But nothing else to speak of."

"Maybe that's because there's nothing else to say."

"I doubt that." His gaze locked on hers, and Ivy's heart stilled. Ivy didn't know why his eyes undid her, but they had a way of diving into her soul. Way down deep.

Their server arrived to clear their dishes. Both declined dessert but accepted coffee.

"I don't mean to press you," he said when their coffees arrived. "You can tell me as little, or as much as, you like."

She stared down into her cup, then back up at him. "I've just always been a very private person."

"Always?" he asked, looking as if he doubted that.

"At least for the past four years."

"You went away to college, didn't you?"

"How did you know that?"

"I picked it up in what Austin said to you."

"You don't miss much."

"I try not to."

She drew a deep breath. "So yeah, I went away to school. Later than most. I was already twenty-one when I started, the age of most students graduating."

"Did you ever think of going straight after high school?"

"Only briefly. I…had my eye on other plans."

"You and Austin were together then?"

"Since our junior year in high school, yeah." She looked at him a little sadly. "We thought we'd work a few years, save up a small nest egg, and then get married. When the bottom fell out, my nest egg went toward something else."

"College tuition," Mark surmised. He surveyed her with compassion. "That was a very brave thing you did. Leaving Rosemont to strike out on your own."

She pushed back in her seat and gave a little laugh. "Didn't last long."

"Lasted long enough. You got your degree, didn't you?"

"Yeah."

"In what?"

"Architectural landscape design."

"Wow. Now it's my turn to be impressed."

"You're teasing me."

"I'm dead serious, Ivy. I may be all about supporting the environment, but I do terrible things to it personally."

"What do you mean?"

"House plants, flower gardens, hedges? None of them would um…consider me a friend. I've got a perpetual brown thumb."

Ivy laughed. "But I've seen your place! The front yard's gorgeous!"

"That's because I just moved in. Give me a month or two. Trust me on this, you'll be horrified."

Ivy shook her head with a chuckle. "For a moment, I was beginning to fear you were prefect."

"Not by a long shot." The waiter brought them their bill, and against Ivy's protests Mark insisted on paying. Once he'd settled up, he turned his gaze on hers. "So what do you plan to do with your degree?"

"Honestly? I have no idea." She studied him a moment while he finished his coffee. "I could give you some pointers, though. On how not to kill your lawn."

"The neighbors would probably appreciate that."

"You don't have any neighbors."

"I was talking about the cows. Even the herd deserves a view."

Ivy laughed. "Yep, they certainly do."

Before they stood, Mark covered her hand with his. "This has been fun, Ivy. I think we should do it again."

"To prepare for the…? Oh my gosh, Mark! We didn't even talk about it!" Ivy checked her watch in a panic. "And now we're out of time. I've gotta dash. I'm running behind."

"Is Eustis really that tough she holds you to the minute?"

"Today she might."

"What's going on?"

Ivy flashed him a grin. "Eustis has a date."

When Ivy got to work, Eustis was flitting about the Coffee Connection like a high-octane firefly. She was moving so fast she nearly collided with Ivy when Ivy stepped behind the counter. "Whoa!" Ivy scooted back a step and out of Eustis's way, as Eustis barreled past, carting a tray full of scones.

"Sorry, doll!" Eustis panted, breathless. "Just trying to finish a few things up."

Ivy took the tray from her. "You go on. I'll take care of this."

Eustis smiled so big her whole brow crinkled. "Seriously?"

"Way seriously." Ivy set the tray on the counter to strap on her apron. She glanced around, seeing that business was slow anyhow. "I'm sorry I'm running late. Mark and I got caught up at—"

"Mark?" Eustis beamed. "Well, well. How did that go?"

"Great." Ivy felt the warmth in her cheeks. "Lunch went great, actually. Mark's not a bad guy."

"Not bad to look at either," Eustis said with a smile.

"Hey!" Ivy play-scolded. "Keep your eyes on your own guy!"

"So, he's *your guy* now, huh?"

Ivy's face steamed. "I never said that."

"In a manner of speaking, you did." Eustis pulled a lipstick from her purse to do a quick touch-up. "Just be careful, all right? He's fresh off the mill, that one."

"Mill?"

Eustis dropped her lipstick back in her bag and lowered her tone. "The marriage mill. He was a runner, remember? And not that long ago."

"Yeah, but maybe he had his reasons." Even though Ivy believed that was true, Eustis's words still niggled at her. Mark had run out on his wedding, just as surely as Austin had run out on theirs. Who knew what Austin had told folks later. Some rumors held he'd blamed it on her.

"Sweetheart," Eustis said. "They *all* have their reasons, some of them better than others."

"So, where are you meeting Walt?" Ivy asked, changing the subject.

"At the La-Tea-Da."

Ivy whistled. That was the fancy place in the Park Hotel that served high tea with linen napkins. It was almost easy to forget Walt Winters was a very rich man. He presented himself so simply, just like a regular Joe. But the word was he was loaded, after having made a mint in oil refining in Texas some time ago. "I thought he was taking you out for java?"

Eustis flushed. "Walt suggested I might like a change of pace."

The rest of the afternoon flew by in a blur for Ivy. Customers came and went, but she could scarcely recall any of their orders. Not that she'd messed up on the job. She'd managed to put it on autopilot. But while her body stayed occupied, her mind was miles away. Already she was concocting ways to restructure Mark's yard. If he was serious about accepting her offer, she could make it a beautiful space. While the landscaping was suitable now, she could think of ways to make it outstanding. The side yard could benefit from a berm of colorful flowers offsetting the mountains. And, in her mind's eye, she could envision the perfect spot under that spreading oak for a two-seater bench. Some place to sit and enjoy the scenery while sipping a glass of wine, or—if Mark preferred—a recyclable bottle of DelaStar draft.

It was amazing to her that Mark could do it. Revitalize a town by repurposing its factory. But she was beginning to believe he could. He'd apparently been successful in other locales, before setting his sights on Rosemont. And the truth was Chicken Fried Foods had already been doomed to fail. Its parent company had pulled out of several locations, without providing alternatives to their dislocated workers. In a way, Mark had arrived just in time. Rather than allowing Chicken Fried Foods to be abruptly closed by its parent company, he'd stepped in like a benevolent rescuer to shut it down gently and ensure a smooth transition to his new operation. Ivy wondered if he might have promised jobs to all those people without her prompting, and suspected he would have. He'd intended to offer everyone a chance at employment anyhow. That was a start, and certainly better than the plans Chicken Fried Foods "corporate" had set in place, which were nonexistent.

Ivy pondered Eustis's cautionary words concerning Mark's reputation as a getaway groom. While there was no denying he'd done it, Ivy still didn't have the full reason why. She hoped that Eustis's intimation was wrong, and that Mark was nothing like Austin. Because, in her heart, Ivy believed the two men couldn't be more different. Austin was a guy who primarily thought of himself. Mark was someone who thought about other people. Wasn't that why he'd guaranteed jobs to all those workers? And also why he did good deeds like ensuring his business contributed in a positive way to the environment?

But there was something more to Ivy's interest in Mark being a genuine stand-up guy. She was starting to like him and didn't want to believe herself a bad judge of character. Not *like* like him! Of course not! Ha-ha. More like *admire-like* him. Yeah, that. It was hard not to be attracted on some level. An intellectual one, at least. Mark was smart, easy-going, and funny. So what if he just happened to have the bluest eyes Ivy had ever seen? Or the face of a big-screen actor? Or…that rock-solid, masculine body? None of those things mattered at all! They were superfluous. Just extras. Bonus accoutrements that would add a nice little touch when he posed as her date at Austin's wedding.

It was one thing to show up with a supposed boyfriend. Or *anti-boyfriend*, which would naturally make everyone think he was the real deal. Quite another to appear with a drop-dead-gorgeous man on her arm, making Ivy the envy of every other woman in town. Ivy considered this a moment, imagining the looks on those female faces. No one in Rosemont had believed Ivy capable of moving on after she'd been ditched at her wedding. Rumors swirled about, saying she was so crushed she'd never be able to fall for another man. Well, she could show them, couldn't she? Show them as well as herself. Even if it was only make-believe, having a pretend date with Mark still represented a new beginning. It provided proof that she could stand up for herself and wasn't afraid to face her former lover, his new fiancée, or anyone else in Rosemont, for that matter. In a weird sort of way, going to Austin's wedding was shaping up to be Ivy's coming-out party. Plus, she was coming into her own. Finally feeling ready to step forward and put certain unsavory parts of her past behind her.

Walt walked Eustis down Main Street to where her house sat near the edge of town. It was at the opposite end from where he lived and the houses were smaller, but Walt admired the quaintness of their structures and the nice way that folks kept their lawns neatly manicured behind white picket fences. When they reached the second to the last gate on the right, Eustis stopped. "This is it," she said with a shrug. "Home, sweet home."

Walt gazed at her, thinking that just about summed it up. He felt comfortable around Eustis, as if he were in the right place at the right time. "It's lovely," he said without taking his eyes off hers. "I like what you've done with the yard."

Eustis blushed. "You're not even looking at the yard."

"Don't need to."

She fiddled with the strap of her purse and studied something imaginary on the sidewalk. When she glanced up, she said, "Thanks for taking me out for tea. It was nice. It was…"

"Refreshing?" he ventured, his brow creasing. Walt hoped his wrinkles didn't betray him, but there was only so much he could do to hide the fact he was pushing sixty. At least twelve years older than Eustis. But maybe, at their age, it didn't so much matter.

"Yeah. Absolutely."

"I hope you didn't think it too forward. My penning that note on the napkin."

She swatted his arm with a laugh. "Don't be silly, old man! I just wondered what took you so long."

Then she turned on her heels and left Walt with his mouth hanging open as she sauntered through the gate.

He swallowed hard and called after her, embarrassed to sound like a kid approaching puberty. "Do it again some time?"

Eustis got to the stoop before turning and crossing her arms in front of her. "Tea, you mean? Don't think so."

Walt's heart sank with a thud, and his belly filled with lead. He was more than an old man. He was an old fool. Imagining someone as young and pretty as Eustis might take an interest...

The next thing he knew, she surprised him with a smile.

"Might consider dinner, though."

Chapter Nine

Mark made his factory rounds early, checking on improvements that had been done and renovations that were still in progress. Everything was coming along, including his settling into Rosemont. The folks he'd guaranteed jobs had appeared genuinely appreciative. Many had assured him he'd made a new friend for life. And somehow he'd believed it. Rosemont didn't seem the sort of town where people said things they didn't mean. Apart from one snaky ex-fiancé of Mark's newfound friend. Whatever Austin had promised Ivy had obviously been a lie. Where was the guy now? Taking up with someone new and about to marry her? Had he stood by his pledge to wed Ivy like an honorable guy? Nope, he hadn't. He'd cut and run just like...

Mark's cheeks sagged at the parallel. Who was *he* to cast stones, when he'd lived in the largest crystal palace of all? Then again, his case was different. Exceptional. Surely, Austin's couldn't have been the same. It was impossible to imagine Ivy catting around on him the way Sandra had cheated on Mark. Besides, Mark could tell from his interactions with Ivy that she considered herself the injured party. Mark stopped walking to wonder whether Sandra had the gall to consider herself the same. *An injured party.* All on account of Mark running out on her.

Mark shoved his hands in his pockets and trudged forward. It didn't matter what Sandra thought. If Mark had that day to do over, his reaction would have been the same. He couldn't stomach Sandra's infidelity, then go on and pretend like nothing had happened. They hadn't even gotten started as husband and wife, and already she'd broken his trust. There wasn't a lot of moving forward from there. Not as far as Mark could see.

His cell buzzed and he checked it, pleased to see the call came from Ivy. "I hope it's not too early?"

"Not early at all," he answered. "Already at work, in fact."

"Good, then you won't mind if I ask your help with something?"

"Anything you need."

"A young man's opinion."

"I thought you considered me mature," he teased.

"You're a spring chicken compared to the guy in question."

"Huh?"

"Walt stopped by the café first thing."

Mark chuckled, trying to imagine where this was going. He recalled Ivy saying that Walt and Eustis had been on a date. "And?"

"He wants to ask Eustis to the wedding."

"Austin's wedding? But I thought the two of them were already invited? I heard Austin ask them myself."

"Separately," Ivy confirmed. "But Walt hopes they can go together. I actually think he's really hung up on her."

Mark grinned. "No way."

"Way," Ivy answered. "And, he's dead serious about not messing it up. Poor thing broke into a sweat. Used up the whole counter dispenser of napkins and everything."

"Whoa."

"That's what I said."

"I'm not getting it. What exactly is it you want me to do?"

She hesitated a moment. "Give him some pointers? Tips for asking a woman out?"

"I'm sure he knows all about that, Ivy. He's been at it longer than I have."

"He's freaked because his grandson's always on the Internet. Told him proposals need to be special nowadays. Not old-school like Walt's used to."

"Proposals? I thought we were talking about—"

"Yeah, yeah. But that's how it is, apparently. Even dates to the prom or homecoming… The girl has got to get asked out in a special way. Something memorable. Picture-worthy."

"Wow. Guess I got off the hook with that one."

"*You* are off the hook because we cut a deal."

"Yeah, I remember."

"Walt's worried that, if he doesn't do this just right, his invite will be a fail."

"It's hard to believe that Eustis is the kind who—"

"Oh, she's up on the whole thing. She's got nieces in high school, you know."

The truth was, Mark didn't, though it hardly mattered. Ivy was asking for his help. And on behalf of Walt. How sweet. While Mark wasn't the biggest Romeo on the block, he likely surpassed many of the fellows in Rosemont in experience. He'd been a big-city bachelor, after all.

Besides, the idea of helping the older lovebirds appealed to something deep in his soul. It felt almost like benefiting the environment. Only better. The prospect of winning points with Ivy tempted too. The more he got to know her, the more he liked her. So contributing to something that would make her friend

Eustis happy would ultimately bring Ivy joy as well. That was, if Eustis was actually into Walt so a date to the wedding with him was what she wanted.

"How do you think Eustis will react to all this?"

Ivy didn't hesitate. "She'll be over the moon."

"And Walt? Does he know that you're talking to me?"

"Who do you think asked me to call?"

That was all Mark needed to hear to ensure his participation.

"Tell me where and when and I'll meet him."

"Oh, that so great, Mark!" Her voice poured sugar sweet through the receiver. "*Thank you.*"

"Any time, Ivy," he said, meaning it. "Any time at all."

Mark met Ivy later that afternoon when she got off work. There was a pretty glow to her cheeks as she met his gaze. "So? How did everything go?"

"Splendid."

They walked away from the Coffee Connection's front window, where Eustis was working inside. "Splendid? What's that mean?"

"Uh-uh," he said with a shake of his head. "These lips are sealed."

"Mark! You can't keep a secret from—"

"Of course I can," he said, grinning. "How do I know you won't squeal?"

"I'll promise!"

"Maybe I don't know you well enough to trust you."

Ivy shoved him in play frustration. "And, maybe I should never have gotten an out-of-towner involved!"

"I'm not an out-of-towner any longer. I've moved in, remember?"

"Yeah, but for how long?"

He stared deep in her eyes, pondering that question, not fully knowing the answer. He liked Rosemont, he did. And he liked the people here—a lot, Ivy in particular. But the truth was, Mark had never stayed in a town once he'd gotten the factory established and his jobs done. Up until now, he'd never seen the point. "For as long as it takes."

"As long as it takes," Ivy repeated. "You're not the kind to let grass grow under your feet, are you?"

"Haven't been until now."

"What makes now different?"

Mark didn't know. But somehow Rosemont *felt* different. Like it was the sort of place he could get used to calling home. The air was clean, the views were spectacular, and the locals were starting to grow on him. Plus, it was only a few hours' drive to the state's capital and largest city. So he could always seek out civilization if he wanted. When he'd thought he'd live here with Sandra, he'd rented the house for a year expressly to try out small-town life. Now that he was back on his own, Mark wondered if it wouldn't be better to return to the life he'd had.

At the moment, though, all Mark wanted was a place with air-conditioning, or a spot in the shade where he could cool down. It was hot as blazes out. "Wanna get some ice cream?" he asked, changing the subject. His gaze darted to the small shop across the way that sold double scoops for the price of one.

Ivy gave a delighted laugh. "I have a better idea."

A short while later, they were seated at a picnic table under the shade of a sprawling tree. Rows of peach trees stretched before them, sidling up to a ridge of the mountains, their limbs hanging heavy with ripe fruit. The orchard stand at their back was rustic, built of logs, and open to the air. More like a covered-porch operation that sold peach everything in summer, including fresh produce by the bushel, pretty jars of preserves, and Ivy's absolute favorite—homemade peach ice cream.

"Mighty good," Mark said, digging his spoon into his cup for another bite.

"Nothing like it when it's hot out," Ivy agreed.

They sat awhile, admiring the view and a pair of parents that had come to harvest peaches with their children.

"Seems like a nice place to bring up kids," Mark commented.

"Yeah. Plenty to do here. Even a Sally hole.

Mark sputtered a laugh. "Sally hole? What's that?"

"It's an old-fashioned word for a swimming hole. There's a great one on the other side of that ridge."

"Filled with cool mountain water?"

"You bet."

He captured her in his gaze. "Sounds enticing."

"I can take you sometime if you'd like."

"No plans this Saturday."

Ivy studied him with a smile. "Are you proposing a date?"

"A pre-wedding one, sure. Why not?"

"Well, I…" Ivy wasn't sure about that. She and Mark pretending to be an item at the wedding was one thing. Lunch at the factory and even ice cream in the afternoon seemed casual. But stripping down into swimsuits together seemed way more personal. Not that she'd totally mind getting a glimpse of Mark in his.

"It's just swimming, Ivy. It's not like you have to worry about me giving you mouth-to-mouth." His eyes sparkled with mischief. "That is, unless you want me to."

"Mark Delacroix!" she snapped back. "You haven't even gotten over your breakup!"

"Who says I haven't?"

"Have you?" she asked, surprised.

"That was four weeks ago."

"Yeah well, mine was six *years* ago, and I'm—"

"Still not over it, are you?"

"What? Well, no. I mean, yes. Of course I'm over it."

"Then what's the problem with the Sally hole?"

She surveyed him with a flush. "You were joking about the—"

"Sweetheart," he said, catching her off guard with the endearment, "I wouldn't bring my lips to yours if you begged me."

Ivy straightened her spine and met his gaze. "Well, don't go holding your breath that I'll start begging any time soon."

Mark dropped his plastic spoon into his empty paper cup. "It sounds like we're on." His mouth curved in a grin. "As long as you can swim, I don't foresee any danger."

All of a sudden, a feeling returned to her. That sensation of ire and aggravation she'd encountered when Mark had first blasted into the Coffee Connection, and not so incidentally, her life. Ivy stood and snatched his empty cup from him, then carted it to a nearby wastebasket with her own and dropped them in.

"I'm sure I swim better than you. I lifeguarded in high school, and also got my certification in CPR."

When she came back to him, he stood to look her in the eye. "Then my heart's in good hands." His mouth hovered over hers, only a fraction of an inch away. He leaned closer, bringing his hand toward her chin.

"Mark," she said a bit breathless, "what are you...?"

Then he dabbed the side of her mouth with a napkin. "Just getting that little speck of ice cream you left behind." His scent washed over her, all masculine and heady, like a spicy musk oil. Ivy's heart beat faster.

"Thanks," she said, still caught up in his gaze. Tingles raced down her spine.

"You will take me swimming? I'd like that very much."

Ivy kicked herself all the way home. She couldn't believe she'd agreed to go swimming with Mark! At the Sally hole, no less! The only good news was that it was typically crowded on Saturdays, with tons of kids and their families. So, it wasn't like she had to worry about her and Mark being alone. When she'd dropped Mark off at his car near the Coffee Connection, there'd been an unmistakable twinkle in his eye as he'd said good-bye. He'd asked where they should meet on Saturday, and whether he should pick her up. But Ivy had insisted on driving, just as she'd suggested she take them to the orchard today. She was the one who knew her way around Rosemont, so that only made sense. In an odd way, Ivy also wasn't sure if she was ready for Mark to see where she lived. Something was happening with Mark. Something Ivy couldn't explain. He'd been relentless in teasing her about the Sally hole. Though she'd picked up early on that teasing was often the same thing as flirting, it was hard to believe Mark had been flirting with her. And, if he had been, toward what end? From all she'd gathered, it wasn't Mark's MO to stick around a town after his setting-up-the-factory job was done.

While Ivy had been getting the vibe from Mark that he was attracted to her, she could hardly see how that mattered. Unless… Ivy slammed a fist against the wheel, thinking what an idiot she'd been. Of course, Mark had been playing up to her, acting all flirty and friendly. That was what their current interactions were supposed to be about. They were priming themselves as a couple to appear genuinely together at Austin's wedding. There was no hidden agenda behind Mark's sultry gazes or tantalizing whispers. It was all part of a great big act for him, and, boy, was he an Oscar winner. Ivy didn't know why she felt mildly disappointed at the realization rather than relieved, but her heart sank just the same. She should be happy, shouldn't she? Glad that Mark was making an effort for the two of them to get along so they'd appear companionable? Besides, it was silly to believe Mark would actually want to kiss her. In actual fact, it was probably the last thing on his mind.

Mark carried a DelaStar draft onto his front porch, unable to get his mind off Ivy. It was bad enough he'd let himself get carried away and had started hitting on her. Then he had to top it off by suggesting he'd like to give her mouth-to-mouth. Counter-suggesting. Basically indicating the opposite of what he burned to do. He took a swig of beer, wrapping his lips around the opening of the bottle. Her mouth had hovered just below his, its warmth only inches away. It would have been easy enough to claim it rather than wipe that imaginary bit of ice cream from her chin. But he'd lost his nerve, and good thing too. What a mess he'd nearly made of things.

Mark strode to the railing, his gaze sweeping the mountains and rolling fields across the way. Rosemont really was scenic. *Bucolic*, a Bostonian might say. And the downtown area, with its broad Main Street and eclectic selection of shops, was both down-home and quaint. He tried to envision what it might have been like living here with Sandra, but somehow he couldn't imagine it. Sandra simply didn't seem like the sort of gal who'd fit into this town. Mark wasn't sure if Rosemont would have liked Sandra much either. The truth was, apart from her other faults, she was also a categorical snob who generally felt herself better than other people. She especially felt that way about people from small towns. *Provincial*, she'd called them, with an upturned tilt to her nose.

Mark had excused her elitism as one of her little quirks. Now, he saw that it was just plain sad. There was so much Sandra missed by not finding value in the basics. Honest work, love of family, a balanced life. The people of Rosemont appreciated those things, and Mark found that refreshing. Just like a dip in a cool mountain lake. Mark thought of him and Ivy at the Sally hole, and grinned in spite of himself. He wondered if the place had a big rope swing like you sometimes saw in movies. The sort you could use to catapult out over the water before letting go—and dropping yourself in. Mark froze, processing the metaphor. In a very large way, he *was* letting go. Letting go of so many things, including his bitterness and hurt over being ditched by Sandra. The truth was, even if she had fit in here, she never could have proved the right match for Mark. He believed that with his whole heart, especially since his heart was telling him there were greener pastures ahead.

Mark didn't know what would happen between him and Ivy. Perhaps nothing beyond a noontime swim and the pretend coupling at Austin's wedding. And maybe that was the way it was meant to be. Mark wasn't sure he was ready to become involved again, and Ivy certainly acted gun-shy. While she'd had plenty of time to move on, she hadn't yet. Mark wondered why, thinking there had to be something more to her story. He wondered if she'd ever trust him enough to share it. Mark studied the view before him, pondering the notion of living here forever. Rosemont would represent a radical change from the big-city world he was used to, but in many respects it might be a welcome change. Mark had been running so hard and so fast his entire life, he'd scarcely had a chance to catch his breath.

He'd come from a modest background, but had guts and determination. He'd also been lucky enough to do well in school and win a scholarship to the Ivy League school where he'd met Sandra. While he'd enjoyed his studies, nothing had fascinated him more than the makings of a business. He'd finished first in his MBA class at age twenty-four, and—by twenty-seven—had made his first million. He'd been able to buy his folks a bigger place and relieve them of the responsibility of ever having to pay a mortgage. Plus, he'd helped his kid sister get her first reliable car, something she needed as a home-based physical therapist. He'd invested too, in retirement plans, stocks, and bonds, and, most importantly, building his business, DelaStar Drafts. He'd diversified enough to weather economic ups and downs, and had managed to keep growing his company as well as his bank account. The truth was, even with all the money DelaStar Drafts contributed to charities and his personal donations each year, Mark had more money than he knew what to do with.

That was leverage Sandra had used when she'd suggested that they marry. Mark had given plenty to his parents and sister; it was time he invest in a family of his own. A wife, two or three kids. A brownstone in town, a summer home in the Hamptons. It had all sounded idyllic and made so much sense. Mark knew children were expensive, and he was determined to raise them right. But just because they grew up rich, that didn't mean they wouldn't understand the value of money. Mark wanted his kids to appreciate and take pride in hard work. Although he was certainly prepared to help them, and would set aside funds for university tuition, he'd expect them to have summer jobs in high school and work during college. It was important to Mark that any offspring of his wouldn't be handed success. They'd have to earn it.

Mark shook his head and took another swig of beer, glad he wouldn't be making those future babies with Sandra. He couldn't fathom what a pain she'd be to the hospital staff, or how demanding she might prove as a mother. She'd probably have to hire a whole roster of nannies just to dole out her numerous perceived responsibilities, when all kids really needed was what Mark had enjoyed: the support of loving parents, and encouragement to work hard and do well. While his parents hadn't been perfect, they'd been good enough to him, and he loved them dearly. His whole family was close, and his sister Diane's boyfriend, Ricky, was a great guy. Everyone loved him and hoped they'd eventually get engaged.

Mark surveyed his near-empty bottle, thinking it would have been better for the world had Diane and Ricky set their nuptials for a month ago rather than him and Sandra. But he supposed those were the breaks. Mark drew a deep breath, taking in the fresh mountain air—cool with the evening and scented with wildflowers. *Letting go*, he reminded himself. That was part of what this time in Rosemont was about. Letting go of the past and moving forward. Even if his stay here turned out to be only temporary, Mark wasn't leaving Rosemont the same guy he was when he got here. He'd be leaving town a new man.

Chapter Ten

Eustis bustled about the coffee shop, preparing to open for the day. Walt was at his customary table in the corner. Normally, Ivy worked Saturdays, but she'd asked Eustis for this morning off. Not that Eustis minded. It wasn't like she had a lot of other stuff to keep her busy. Other than attending her grandkids' soccer games, her weekends stayed pretty quiet. And soccer was out of season. She glanced at Walt a moment, thinking something about him seemed off. Of course, it was hard to tell with that splayed newspaper covering his face and half the table. Must be a mighty interesting edition today.

"Want something?" she asked from the counter.

Walt rattled the paper and kept reading. "I'll wait."

Now Eustis *knew* something was up. Walt could barely ever wait on his coffee. In fact, he practically demanded it first thing. Sometimes he even played snarky cranky if he didn't get it fast enough, though both she and Ivy understood Walt's bark was worse than his bite. "Suit yourself!" She turned back to her work of stocking the pastry case, another thought occurring. Perhaps Walt wasn't feeling well. Hadn't he made a beeline for the bathroom first thing? She wasn't even sure how long he'd been in there. One minute he was gone, then, by the time she'd set up the tables, he'd suddenly reappeared in the corner and settled in while her back was turned. Eustis got a feeling in her gut something funny was going on, but she hadn't a clue what.

The door chime tinkled, and a couple of morning regulars sauntered in. The town fire chief, Josh, with one of his senior volunteers, Caleb. Rosemont was too small to staff a paid station. They didn't even have a police officer. Instead, the greater county's sheriff looked after them. Not that much ever happened in Rosemont requiring police intervention.

"Mighty hot today," Josh said by way of greeting.

Eustis smiled at him and Caleb as they took a table near the front. Caleb tugged off his firefighter hat. "Think I'll take my coffee ice-cold."

"You boys been out already?" Walt inquired from behind his paper.

"Well, howdy, Walt!" Josh said. "Almost didn't see you there."

"He's been making himself nearly invisible," Eustis said in a whisper.

"We had a call," Josh answered loudly. "Turned out to be a false alarm."

"Cat up a tree," Caleb said.

"Right," Josh replied. "Two of them."

Eustis's eyebrows shot up as two women breezed in the door.

"Wicked hot out there," Delilah said, fanning her face with her purse. Delilah worked at the bakery down the street and was generally occupied at this time in the morning. Eustis puzzled at her being here with her sister, Betty, who worked with her. "You ladies closed today?" Eustis asked them.

Betty flashed her a grin. "Just for a bit."

"That's right," Delilah said. "We thought we'd take a coffee break."

Eustis stared out the front window, her jaw dropping. Here came Hank from the bank. And Georgia, the florist from the stand on the corner. Wait a minute! Was that Ivy's cousin Grace from the paper scurrying after her? Eustis thought she took the weekend shift. Wasn't *anybody* working today?

Before Eustis knew it, the Coffee Connection was packed. She'd never seen so many people here! What a fine day for Ivy to take off! She hurried about, taking orders and filling coffees. The whole while, Walt and his paper didn't budge. Then suddenly there was a crinkling sound, and the room gave a collective gasp. Eustis stared straight at Delilah, who brought her hand to her heart as if she'd just seen the most darling thing. Caleb chuckled and shot his gaze across the room at Walt. "I think someone's trying to tell you something."

Eustis turned Walt's way and saw he'd flipped his paper upside-down. But wait! There was something written on the back. Something penned in huge black letters in what appeared to be permanent marker. Only it looked like Chinese.

Walt held the paper tightly, his knuckles turning white, as Josh furiously motioned for him to flip it upside-down. Walt glanced down, his whole face reddening when he saw his message was inverted. Carefully turning the paper around, he held it toward Eustis, who just stared like he'd arrived from Mars. In giant black letters, the words read, *Wedding Date?*

Eustis set a hand on her hip and cocked an eyebrow at Walt. "What's this about?"

He swallowed hard, his Adam's apple rising. "Two weeks from today," he said. "Austin and Caroline's wedding. I mean, I could go alone, but I really wouldn't want to. What I mean is, it would make me very honored to have a stunning redhead on my arm."

Eustis's skin burned hot from her head to her toes as the whole room looked on. Then Walt stunned her further by lowering the paper. Behind it, she saw what he'd been hiding: a spectacular vase of sunflowers! He titled his head with a grin. "They reminded me of you."

"What?" Eustis asked, nearly speechless.

The café patrons watched, holding their collective breath. It suddenly occurred to Eustis why the place was so crowded. Word must have spread about Walt's plan, and these busybody townsfolk had to see for themselves if the rumor was true. Not that Eustis really minded busybodies. Most of the time, she was one herself.

"Do you think for a minute," Walt asked her, "that the only reason I come here every morning is for coffee?"

Eustis pursed her lips, unsure of what to say.

"Say yes!" Delilah urged. Others voiced their agreement, egging Eustis on.

Only she didn't need extra convincing. She'd never had anyone on the planet do something like this for her. It wasn't just a surprise, it was sweet. Extra sweet. A charming gesture from a charming man. And he'd put himself out there too, his heart and his hopes right on the line. That was plenty special.

"Well…?" Walt asked, his voice a slight stammer. "Will you go?"

Eustis folded her arms in front of her as Walt watched with hopeful dark eyes.

"Why Walt," she said with a saucy lilt. "I'd be delighted."

Then the entire café broke into applause, as somewhere in the background a flashbulb popped.

Chapter Eleven

Mark checked the clock in Ivy's car against the time on his cell and grinned. "Should be just about over."

Ivy shot him a sideways glance, then set her gaze back on the winding country road. "What should be over?"

They were headed up to Cool Springs at the foot of Sugar Mountain. She was wearing cut-off jean shorts and a T-shirt over what appeared to be a bikini underneath, and she couldn't have looked cuter. Mark just wore his swim trunks with a polo. He'd thrown a change of clothes in a bag, because he wasn't sure how long they intended to stay or what their plans might be afterward.

He sat back in his seat, adjusting the shoulder strap. "Walt's big ask."

Ivy nearly veered off the road. "Mark! It's today? You didn't breathe a word!"

"You didn't ask."

"Most certainly did. Only about a billion times."

"Well, okay, Walt wanted to keep it a secret."

"It's hard to keep much of anything quiet in Rosemont."

"Nobody else knew about this plan," he said, filling her in.

After he'd supplied the details, Ivy giggled. "I wish I could have seen Eustis's face. I'll bet she was floored."

"Floored but flattered, right? You did say you could pretty much guarantee she would go."

"Oh yeah. Truth is, I think she's had a secret crush on Walt for some time. She's always making comments about how he looks like an old sea captain, but in a good way. Quipping about how back in the day, she'd bet he had a girl in every port."

"You think he was that much of a player?"

"Hardly. He was married to his late wife, Mary, for over thirty years. But that Eustis has an imagination. Maybe she's been imaging she was one of those girls in those many ports."

Mark chuckled.

"Here's what I don't get," Ivy told him. "How'd he bring that big vase of flowers in without Eustis seeing it? She must have let him in the shop."

"Made arrangements with Georgia to hand them through the bathroom window."

"Georgia? The-florist-on-the-corner Georgia?" Ivy sputtered a laugh. "Now I *know* Walt's little proposal wasn't kept secret."

"How can you say that?"

"Georgia Thurston's the biggest blabbermouth in town. For all we know, all of Rosemont appeared to watch the show."

Mark wrinkled his brow in surprise. "You think?"

"I'd lay money on it," Ivy said with a nod.

"Well, I hope that didn't discourage Walt."

"I doubt Walt discourages that easily," Ivy said.

"No, I suppose he wouldn't. Not after he'd already gone to the trouble. I hope Eustis didn't mind the surprise."

"I'm sure she loved it." Ivy's cheeks colored slightly. "What woman doesn't like being surprised with flowers?"

Ten minutes later, they pulled into a gravel parking area hedged with honeysuckle bushes. They were near the foot of the mountain, and Mark could hear gurgling waters and the sounds of happy children shouting and splashing outside his rolled-down window. He turned to Ivy before she could exit the car. "Thanks for bringing me here."

"Glad to."

"You didn't seem so sure about it when I suggested the invitation."

Bangs grazed dark eyebrows framing chocolate-colored eyes. "You were very insistent."

"It's good to go swimming in summertime."

"Yeah, but…" Her words fell off, and she pursed her lips.

"But what?"

"The thing is, I haven't done this in a while. Come out to the Sally hole, I mean."

"How come?"

"I don't know. In some ways, it's kid's stuff."

"And in others?"

She stared out the windshield, apparently pained by a memory.

"Ivy?" Mark asked softly.

After a long pause, she finally answered. "I used to come out here with Austin in high school."

Now Mark felt horrible for forcing an invitation. "You should have said something."

"It's all right." She met his gaze. "Really. That was a long time ago."

He reached up and stroked her cheek, finding it damp. "A lifetime ago, Ivy. You're a different person now."

"You're right," she said bravely. "And in this case, different is good."

"Sure looks that way from where I sit."

She blushed and hung her head. "You're just being nice again. Flirting."

Mark swallowed hard, because she'd nailed him. In a way, he probably was. But it was impossible not to say kind things to Ivy. Particularly since she deserved them and had no business feeling bad over some jerk who'd jilted her years ago. Mark gently lifted her chin to look in her eyes. "I call things how I see them. And I'm a very good judge of character."

"Except for that one time."

He could have taken that to heart, but instead he chuckled. He wasn't mad at Ivy for mentioning Sandra. This seemed to be a conversation about exes, after all. "You've got me there."

She sucked in a breath, apology lining her face. "I'm sorry, I shouldn't have mentioned—"

"It's okay. I'm over it."

"Already?"

"Absolutely. Once I thought things out, I understood that Sandra and I not being together was for the best. For a lot of people."

"What do you mean?"

"It doesn't matter," he told her, deciding that it didn't. There was no reason for Ivy to know Mark had considered making babies with Sandra, before he'd grasped how wrong building a future and a family with her would be. "So!" he said, nabbing his towel off the backseat. "We going to do this thing or not?"

Ivy grabbed her towel too, then sprang from the car. "Last one there's a rotten egg!"

"Hey! I don't even know where—" he called, chasing after her.

Ivy giggled and glanced over her shoulder before running faster.

It looked like Mark was just going to have to race after her and find out.

Ivy paused when they got to the clearing. Mark stood beside her, panting, his broad chest heaving below the cornflower-blue polo that complemented his eyes. "Wow," he said, looking around. He was clearly awed by the crystal-clear basin, shaded by evergreens on one side and bordered by large flat rocks on the other that loaned themselves to sunbathers. Beyond them, waters tumbled down the side of the mountain, cascading over craggy rocks, before finally pooling in the Sally hole. A large tree on the shady side even held a huge rope swing, draped from a sturdy branch. Some kids were using it now to catapult themselves out over the water before letting go and dropping in, hollering as they fell.

"Looks like fun," Mark said. He pulled off his shirt, and Ivy's pulse quickened. His chest was even more spectacular without the shirt on, musculature rippling beneath a dark smattering of hair. It trailed in a perfect "V" from his pecs down to his navel, disappearing beneath the waistband of his swim trunks.

Ivy swallowed hard, her face burning hot when he caught her looking. She averted her gaze, then spoke with an embarrassed squeak. "Let's find a place to put our towels."

Mark studied her with amusement. "All right."

"Sun or shade?" she asked him.

He surveyed the scene before deciding. "How about we claim one of those rocks over there?"

"Sounds great."

"Did you wear sunscreen?" he asked, apparently concerned because she was fair.

"Plenty. And you?"

"Packed some in my bag." He smiled. "Maybe you can help me put some on?"

"Sure," she said, like that was the most natural thing in the world, her laying her hands all over Mark's red-hot body. Okay. So, not *all over*. He'd probably just need help with his back. But that was bad enough. Ivy hadn't been up close and personal with a man in… Well, anyhow. Far too long. The dates she'd had since Austin had never panned out. Whenever the kissing had started to lead to something more, Ivy had pulled back. Then, she'd never seen that guy again. Ivy knew far too well the dangers involved in becoming physical. And the outcome could be devastating.

"You all right?" Mark asked, noting her frown. He'd already laid his towel on the rock and now offered to help with hers. She handed him one edge of it, and they stretched it out together, flattening it against the rock next to Mark's.

Ivy forced her face to brighten. "Yeah, fine. Need help with that?" she asked, seeing he'd pulled out his sunscreen. To her mild disappointment, it was the spray-on kind. Ivy wouldn't be touching Mark's body at all.

"If you don't mind? Just a little on my shoulders?"

Mark sat on his towel, and Ivy spritzed him, thinking what solid shoulders Mark had. Big enough to take on a lot of troubles. Yet likely not broad enough to take on hers. She sighed, feeling foolish. What was she thinking of doing? Telling Mark about her past?

She finished with the sunscreen and sat next to him when he thanked her. They both watched the others for a while. Young couples frolicking in the water, kids splashing each other's faces…

"Aren't you going to take that off?" Mark asked Ivy regarding her tank top. But Ivy wasn't sure how exposed she wanted to be. On a lot of levels.

"I'm good."

Mark shrugged. "As long as you're not too hot."

Ivy wasn't sure why, but she felt driven to open up to this man. She needed to tell him things she'd said to very few others. She didn't know if it was because Mark was kind to her, or because she knew he'd eventually be leaving town. It was likely a combination of both. Sort of like making a confession to a sympathetic stranger on an airplane.

Mark noted her distant look. "Something's bothering you. I wish you'd tell me what. If it's Austin, and coming here is too—"

"It is Austin," she said without looking at him, "but maybe not in the way you think."

"I'm sorry, Ivy. We can go," he said, starting to stand.

She laid her hand on his arm.

"No, let's stay. There's something I need to tell you."

He met her gaze and picked up on something. "If it's personal, you don't have—"

"It's about Austin. About our wedding."

"The one that wasn't," he said.

"Yes." She swallowed hard and turned away. When she turned back to him, she felt heat in her eyes.

"He ran out on me. Left me standing at the altar. You know that."

Mark's temples colored. "I put some of that together."

"But he had a reason just like you did."

Mark's jaw dropped. "I can't believe that's true. That you'd—"

"I didn't play around on him, if that's what you mean."

He studied her with sympathy.

"It's what I told him before the ceremony that made him go."

Kind blue eyes sparkled in the sunlight, picking up the reflection of the water.

"You don't have to tell me."

"I know, but I want to."

Mark reached out and took her hand. "Then I'm here."

"He... I..." Ivy's lips trembled. Her voice cracked as she said it. "I was pregnant, Mark."

He studied her a beat, then spoke gently.

"That must have been very hard."

"We were both barely twenty."

His face registered understanding. "Is that why you...? You and Austin decided to marry?"

Ivy nodded and wiped back a tear with a sniff. "Only, it didn't take."

His face registered concern. "What didn't?"

She tightened her grip on his hand. "The baby."

Mark stared at her with incredulity. "You're not saying that—"

"I lost the baby before the wedding. Miscarried. Once Austin found out our getting hitched was no longer necessary, he..." Her words dissolved into sobs.

Mark released her hand and wound his arms around her, pulling her close.

He hugged her to him, saying hoarsely, "Austin was a first-class jerk. I hope you know that."

She nodded, weeping against his shoulder, her tears mixing with coconut-scented sunscreen. Mark held her tighter and gently stroked her hair. "Who else knows?"

"Only Eustis. But I'm sure there were rumors."

"That's part of why you left, isn't it?" he asked with gentle understanding.

"Yes."

"But you came back. Why?"

She pushed back to look at him. "Because I realized I couldn't run forever."

"Nobody can," he agreed. "It's exhausting."

Ivy felt as if her heart might burst at any moment at the hurtful memory.

"You know what I think?"

"What?" Her voice came out in a warble.

"I think it's time you left Austin behind you." His eyes brimmed with encouragement and understanding. "And I'm going to help you do it."

"How?"

His gaze darted to the rope swing across the way. Then he stood, taking her hand. "Come on. I have an idea."

They had to wait in line behind a string of little kids, but finally it was their turn.

"You sure about this?" Ivy asked.

"Dead-set positive. Only… One quick practical question. Do you think it will hold us?"

Ivy's eyes brightened. "It holds Big Bubba."

"Who's Big Bubba?"

"Three hundred and fifty pound former football player."

Mark laughed. "Excellent! Then grab on!"

Ivy looked at him askance. "You want to do this together?"

"Yes."

"Why?"

"Because this old bear here," he said, shaking the braided rope, "is like Austin. In fact, it's a lot like Sandra too. And probably a bunch of other unsavory exes out there, all tangled up together."

Ivy smiled, her cheeks going dusty rose. "We're letting go, aren't we?"

"I sure as hell hope so." He wrapped his arms around her and clung to a high part of the rope, centering his hands above where she'd placed hers. She was in front of him now, still in her cut-offs and tank top. But Mark realized it really didn't matter. What counted was what they were about to do. "On three, Ivy. Are you ready?"

She nodded, leaning back into him as they gathered leverage to swing forward. The next thing Mark knew, they were flying out over the water. It was now or never. They had to let go. There was no time for *One* or *two*. "Three!" Mark suddenly shouted. Ivy released the rope just when he did with a cry of glee. "Wheeeee!"

"Whoohoo!" Mark joined her, their voices echoing off the mountain.

Then *whoosh!* He got sucked into water so icy cold it took his breath away. Mark kicked up to the surface to find Ivy already wading there, laughing. "That was *awesome!*" she said, her cheeks bright pink.

"Yeah," he agreed. "Pretty amazing."

Ivy swam to the bank, then stripped off her tank top and shorts, exposing her dynamite figure. She was so smoking hot, Mark had to dip his head back under the water just to cool off. "Want to go again?" Ivy called from the shore.

"Right with you!" he answered, swimming as fast as he could.

The two of them laughed all the way back to Mark's place. What a great time they'd had. Especially once the little kids had been called home for supper, and they no longer had to wait in line for the swing. Ivy couldn't remember when she'd had such a fun day or when her spirit had felt so free. Part of that came from confessing her secret and another part from finally letting go. Yes, *letting go* of that scumbag Austin. She didn't know why she'd let his memory have so much influence over her for so long. But the important thing was that it was done. Ivy believed that in the recesses of her soul. Austin had finally been exorcised. And Mark Delacroix had a lot to do with that.

"I want to thank you," she said, when they got back to his house. "Thank you for everything, and for such a great day."

"Thank *you* for taking me to the Sally hole."

"It was a good idea."

"The best."

Mark gathered his things and stepped from the car. Ivy's heart sank just a tad to think their outing was over. But what did she imagine? They'd already spent the whole day together. It wasn't like they would spend the night together too. "Thanks for driving," he said before shutting his door.

Ivy nodded, then sadly watched him walk toward his house until he stopped suddenly and turned on his heels. She eyed him curiously as he returned to her car with purposeful strides and stopped outside her open driver-side window. "I'm sorry," he said, blue eyes twinkling. "Forgot something."

Ivy couldn't imagine what that might be. He already had his bag and towel. Then he slowly lowered his head, leaning in above her door. "This," he said in a gravelly whisper. Ivy titled up her chin, unable to believe what was happening. But she wanted it to happen. Oh yes, she did. His lips met hers and felt like heaven, with just the sweetest hint of pressure. He gave her another light kiss, then pulled back with a smile.

"I'm looking forward to that wedding."

"Me too," she answered, a million wild butterflies fluttering inside her.

"Call you in the meantime?"

Ivy's heart hammered harder beneath her shoulder harness. "You'd better."

Mark stroked her cheek good-bye. "Count on it."

Chapter Twelve

When Ivy arrived at the Coffee Connection on Monday to open up, Walt was standing there, whistling.

"Morning, Walt," Ivy told him. "You seem cheerful."

Once she'd let him indoors, he surprised her with a grin. "Made the morning paper!"

Ivy stared at the edition he fanned open before her. Sure enough, it was Walt! Sitting there at his customary table with a big vase of sunflowers. The foreground showcased a nice big wedge of someone's backside. "Is that Eustis?"

"Good angle."

"Not sure what she'll have to say about that."

"Not sure who will have to say about what?" Eustis asked, entering behind them. She stared down at Walt's paper. "Heavens to Betsy! Is that *me*?"

Walt looked at her, his face flushing crimson. "I think it's cute."

"Cute?" Eustis stammered. "Who on earth took that picture?"

"Must have been Grace," Walt informed her.

Eustis nodded, seeming to recall she'd been there. "Well, I guess we've been outed," she said, meeting Walt's gaze.

"Good!" he said. "I'd hate other guys in town to think you were available. Especially after all the positive press." He indicated the photo, and Eustis blinked.

Ivy strapped on her apron. "Sounds like I missed a lot of excitement around here."

"The place was packed," Eustis said.

"Yep," Walt agreed. "You'd think someone sold tickets."

"No one needs tickets when Georgia's involved," Eustis quipped.

They all laughed lightly, knowing it was true.

"She means well," Ivy said.

"Of course she does," Eustis said. "Well enough not to want to leave anybody out when she smells news."

Walt took his seat with a grin. "Even called a reporter!"

Eustis shook her head and started making Walt's coffee. "I suppose one good thing came out of it."

Walt and Ivy turned to her.

She surprised them with a sassy smile. "I got a date to Austin's wedding."

"Speaking of dates," Eustis whispered to Ivy, "how did yours go with Mark?" The café had begun to fill with regular weekly patrons, though Ivy suspected that it wasn't nearly as slammed as it had been on Saturday.

"It wasn't a date, exactly."

"No?" Eustis studied her. "What exactly *was* it?"

"We just went swimming, Eustis."

"I'll bet your eyes were *swimming* all over that physique of his."

"Shush!" Ivy hissed under her breath. "Someone will hear you."

As if to prove her point, she noted several heads swiveled in their direction.

"Your orders are coming right up!" Eustis told them. "No need to get nosy!"

Walt chuckled in the corner and rattled the paper in front of him. Almost sounded like he mumbled *that's my girl*.

Eustis scooted toward Ivy as she poured two coffees. "So?" she asked. "What was it like? That beefcake bod." Green eyes twinkled. "Up close and personal?"

Ivy turned away with a flush. "Wouldn't know."

"Sweet cherry pie!" Eustis whispered back. "He kissed you, didn't he?"

Ivy peered back over her shoulder. "How did you…?"

Eustis's lips twisted in a grin. "It's written all over your face."

Ivy dropped her chin to hide her cheeks that were burning hotter. "Might have given me a little peck."

"Aha!"

"Just one."

"Hmm," Eustis replied, like she doubted it.

"All right, already. Maybe two. But the second hardly counted it was so quick. And through the driver's side window."

"*What?*" Eustis shouted just a little too loudly.

"*Eustis*…" Ivy warned.

"Coffee?" a customer grumpily reminded them.

"Go grind your own darn beans!" Eustis snapped back. She blinked at Ivy, then brought her hand to her mouth in a giggle. "Whoops. I said that out loud, didn't I?" Then she scurried to her customer with the coffee pot. "My apologies, sir." She heaved a breath and glanced at Walt, who sat there grinning at her like the proudest man on earth. "Seriously didn't mean to say that! The tab's on me."

Mark made his rounds at the factory, pleased to see everything coming along. The large plate-glass window facing the sandwich shop would go in Friday. Preliminary plant operations would start next week. They'd be fully operational by the end of the summer. When Mark had planned to marry Sandra and stay awhile, he'd rented his cottage for a year. Now, he wondered if he shouldn't have let it month-to-month like he'd done his previous places in the other towns where he'd set up DelaStar Drafts. His typical pattern was to stay in a place to oversee hiring and renovations for the new plant, then to return to Boston, where he still kept a brownstone. He'd make periodic trips to the sites afterward, to perform quality control checks, and ensure all went smoothly.

Mark sensed a tug in his heart at the thought of moving away. He'd had an incredible time with Ivy at the swimming hole and really looked forward to seeing her again. But could he really envision upending his whole existence by relocating permanently to Rosemont? In one sense, he believed that building a new beginning in someplace like Rosemont would be good for him. In another, he wasn't certain he was prepared to make such a huge transition. And yet, here he was, sinking in deeper with Ivy. Maybe even getting in over his head.

He hadn't intended to kiss her good-bye on Saturday, but when he'd gotten halfway to his stoop, he'd felt compelled to turn around. It was like Ivy was a magnet and he couldn't resist her pull, or the beckoning of those sweet-as-sugarcane lips. It had been a chaste kiss, but its impact had sent current ricocheting to Mark's spine. He'd been tempted to take Ivy from that car and hold her. Draw her body up against his in a sweeping embrace. Then he might have kissed her more deeply and with all the passion he could offer. Mark was surprised to find those fires reigniting so quickly after his disaster with Sandra. But the truth was, everything about Ivy felt different. Because she was different. Radically different from Sandra. So in every way his emotions concerning her were distinct.

Ivy was sweet and sensitive, with a good sense of humor and a kind, giving soul. And, she could fill out a bikini like nobody's business. Mark hated that Austin had treated her so badly. She'd explained more fully that she hadn't even miscarried the baby until the night before the wedding. She'd been unable to reach Austin from the hospital, as he'd been pulling an all-night drunk at a rowdy bachelor party. When she'd finally confronted him with the truth on the morning of their wedding, he hadn't taken it badly on the surface. In fact, he'd assured her he still loved her and that it didn't make a difference.

Oddly, Austin never expressed remorse over losing the baby, and that knowledge pained Ivy still, making her wonder what kind of father he might have been. In any case, she'd never have the opportunity to find out. After swearing it didn't matter and that he'd still be there, Austin had changed his mind halfway to the altar and bolted. He'd only told Eustis later why he'd done it, after Eustis chased him down and demanded an explanation. She'd found him at a corner bar nursing his second beer, and it wasn't even eleven o'clock. He'd said since Ivy was no longer knocked up, it wasn't really necessary. Ivy thought Eustis might have slapped him then, but Eustis wouldn't say. She did rub her red palm a lot for the rest of the morning, though.

Mark shoved his hands in his pockets and headed back to his office, thinking the sentiment he'd expressed to Ivy was spot-on. Austin really *had* been a first-class jerk. And maybe still was. Then again, people changed, and the truth was Austin might have had the opportunity to grow up. For Caroline's sake, Mark certainly hoped so. It was funny how the whole town was turning out for the wedding. But, apparently, in Rosemont, that was how things were done. Folks supported the nuptials of even their frenemies, Mark supposed, in part, because none of the people here could bear to miss out. If something was happening in Rosemont, everyone had to be in on it.

This just underscored what an outsider Mark had been when he'd prepared to marry Sandra. While they'd attempted to include a few townsfolk in their efforts toward positive PR, all had politely declined the invitation. Mark understood now that was because he and Sandra had been viewed as outsiders. Not only that, everyone was skeptical of Mark because they believed him primed to ruin the town. Shut down their one remaining factory, and put the populace out of work. Mark hoped by now he'd been able to disabuse folks of that notion. Ivy, Eustis, and Walt appeared to be helping his cause, and Ivy's cousin Grace had begun to write much more flattering columns in the paper. Mark was grateful to them, every one. He wasn't as hard-nosed a businessman as some people suspected. It mattered to Mark what people thought of him *and* his enterprise. He'd worked hard to build a brand for DelaStar Drafts, and he understood that the reputation of the man behind it was just as important. But of all the folks in Rosemont, Ivy's opinion of him mattered most. He wanted her to believe he was a really good guy, and needed her to understand he was *nothing* like Austin. Even if Mark had run out on his own wedding too, that didn't mean that he and Austin had anything else in common. In many ways they seemed as different as Sandra and Ivy.

Mark entered his office and sank down in his chair. He didn't know where things were going with Ivy. Just as he couldn't foresee where the future might see him a month from now. For the time being, he was here in Rosemont and determined to make the best of it. Including his budding friendship with a sweet Southern gal. Mark ran a hand through his hair, shaking off the notion that the word *friendship* felt wrong. But they *were* just friends, weren't they? Hadn't that been part of their deal?

Mark turned his chair to the window facing the sandwich shop across the street, recalling his and Ivy's lunch there. His mind flashed back to the disastrous scene of him skidding into the Coffee Connection for the first time and landing at Ivy's feet behind the counter… Then forward to the mesmerizing moment he'd felt driven to kiss her good-bye. In between, there'd been rope swinging and laughter, and a whole lot of letting go. Mark's insides turned over as he realized what was happening. In spite of himself, he was falling for Ivy Green.

Chapter Thirteen

Mark called Ivy later that day to see how her morning shift at gone at the café and ask whether she'd spoken to Eustis. He was pleased Eustis seemed happy with Walt's invitation, and that the two had some sort of flirtation going on. At any age, that was sweet. But it somehow appeared extra special for Walt and Eustis. Each had lost their spouse and been alone for some time. It was funny what the fates sometimes had in store. It brought a smile to Mark's lips, thinking he'd had a hand in helping shape that happy outcome.

"How did you know about the sunflowers?" Ivy asked. "That those were her favorites."

"I didn't," Mark said. "But I told Walt to ask Georgia."

"Smart man."

He chuckled. "Georgia told him Eustis always admired her sunflowers, said they reminded her of Italy."

"Italy?" Ivy laughed. "I don't think she's ever been."

"Maybe Walt will take her there on her honeymoon," Mark teased.

"Aren't you getting a little ahead of yourself?"

"They *are* going to a wedding together, Ivy."

"Yeah," she said happily, "and so are we."

Ivy couldn't think of anyone she'd rather have take her. She and Mark had had such a great time on Saturday, and his kiss had rocked her world. It was like she could truly appreciate it, because she was no longer thinking of Austin. How stupid of her that she'd let that get in the way with every other guy. With Mark, it had been all about him. It was impossible to imagine being with anyone else. Particularly after seeing him in swim trunks, Ivy thought with a giggle.

"It will be a good time," he answered. Mark paused before continuing gently. "You're no longer worried about Austin?"

"Not a bit."

"Great, because you shouldn't be."

"Thanks, Mark. For the rope swing. For everything."

"It was good for me too."

She laughed. "I thought you were already over Sandra?"

"I was. But now I'm double over her. Triple even."

Ivy felt herself grin. "I'm so glad."

"You helped me too, Ivy. Just being in Rosemont has."

"It's a nice town."

"I think so."

"That's why you came back here?"

"This is home. It's what I know."

"Ever think of going anywhere else?"

"I moved away for college."

"I meant, besides that."

"Not really. My roots are here."

"Roots and family?"

"Eustis is my family."

"You're parents aren't—"

"Eustis was my mom's best friend. Lost my dad in a car accident. And Mama to cancer a few years later. Eustis took me in my senior year of high school."

"I'm sorry, Ivy," he said sadly. "I didn't know."

"You couldn't have."

"Want to meet up after work? For coffee or something? Maybe a drink?"

"I'd love to, but I'll be at the library later."

"Hitting the books? But I thought you were done with—"

"Not studying. Planting." Suddenly, she got an idea. Mark was big and strong, with a lot of muscle in his back. "Want to come help me dig?"

A few hours later, Mark stopped by his house to change into jeans and a T-shirt. What Ivy had suggested sounded like hot work, but Mark didn't mind getting his hands dirty. He was happy to help out with Ivy's project. *Commons Area Beautification*, she called it. He chuckled to himself that it sounded mighty upscale, but he stopped laughing the minute he got to the library. Mark pulled into the small parking area, then stared in awe at the stunning flowerbeds Ivy was putting in. She waved him over with a smile, wearing cut-off shorts, a tank top, and sturdy garden gloves.

"This is amazing," he said, noting she'd placed the pots in the exact locations where she intended to plant them.

"A couple of shade trees will go over there." She indicated the far side of the small brick building with tall white columns. "I've planned a flagstone path leading from the book-drop window to that area where two benches will go under the trees."

Mark surveyed the mountains beyond the building, imagining how brilliantly those hills must bloom with autumn color in the fall, and deep fragrant greens in springtime. "Looks like the perfect spot for outdoor reading. Especially in the fall and spring."

Her eyes lit up. "That's just what I was thinking!" She dug her shovel into the ground so it stayed, then pulled some sort of blueprints from her pocket. "This is my master plan."

Mark took the paper in his hands and studied it. "This is going to be some transformation."

"Hope so!" Her cheeks glowed bright pink and her brow was dabbed with moisture, but she looked happy.

"I knew you said you'd studied landscape architecture, but I didn't know you worked freelance."

"I don't," she said with a shrug. "This is volunteer work, but I'd *love* to make a job of it someday." Her eyes shone brightly. "Wouldn't that be cool?"

"Very," he agreed. "But if this is volunteer, then who's covering the costs?"

"Oh, that!" She laughed lightly. "It's my time that's volunteered. The town did a fundraiser to pay for supplies. I think it will be worth it, don't you?"

"One hundred percent."

Mark couldn't help but think how much Ivy seemed in her element. She appeared to love working outdoors, in spite of the afternoon heat. And her plan for the grounds was fantastic. She was not only enthusiastic about this work, she was obviously very talented too. He handed back her blueprints with a smile.

"Why don't you tell me what I can do to help."

"How good are you with a shovel?" she asked, handing it to him.

"Probably a lot better than I am with a broom."

Ivy met his gaze, and her lips pulled into a smile. "I thought you did okay cleaning up."

Mark's heart stilled, remembering that earlier moment in the café, when he'd scarcely been able to take his eyes off her. Mostly because he feared she was about to clobber him senseless. "I'll try not to make such a mess here."

"Your track record's improving." She pointed to a couple of small trees in the back of a pickup. "If you wouldn't mind carrying those up the hill before you start digging?"

"Just tell me where you want everything to go."

Mark and Ivy stayed busy until the sun sank low and nearly all the planting was complete. There were just a few more rows of pansies to go in by the daffodils lining the walk, and Ivy said she could handle that herself tomorrow. Mark had already done the heavy lifting and laid down the flagstone path to the shade trees. The nursery was bringing the outdoor benches over to install at the end of the week, at no cost.

"Thanks for your help, Mark. I never could have gotten this done without you. Certainly not in one day."

"I was happy to help out."

She studied him, considering something. "I'm meeting up with my cousin later tonight, but tomorrow's open if you're free?"

"What did you have in mind?"

"My homemade spaghetti dinner. Made with fresh garden herbs," she tempted him.

Mark couldn't think of anything he'd like better. "Sounds delicious. I'll bring the wine."

"Not some DelaStar drafts?"

He shook his head with a laugh. "A nice Chianti would probably work better."

Ivy strode to the pickup truck and pulled a pen and notepad from its glove box, offering to write down her address.

"You're driving this truck?" Mark asked, surprised. "What happened to your car?"

"It's back at my place. I keep Chevonne here for the dirty work."

Mark studied the rusty hubcaps and beat-up fenders of the well-worn machine. There were dents in the doors, and paint was chipping off the hood, where the truck had apparently been hard-dinged by hail. "Chevonne?"

"It's an old Chevy. Used to belong to my dad. I named her back in high school. She's a little road weary, but she still gets the job done."

He held open her driver's door, and she climbed into the cab. "So…" She gave a little shrug. "Guess I'll see you tomorrow?"

Mark couldn't believe how cute she looked sitting there in that beat-up old truck. But somehow it suited her.

"Yeah." He stepped forward before she could shut the door. "But, first…"

She paused to stare at him. There was no one else in the parking area, as the library had closed an hour before.

"How do you feel about kissing a sweaty old guy?"

Ivy laughed and spun in her seat to face him, her knees grazing the front of his jeans. "You're not so old," she said, wrapping her arms around his neck.

Mark tugged her to him and pulled her into an embrace. Suddenly they were face-to-face and chest to chest, her wickedly warm body pressed to his. Mark's heart pounded furiously beneath his damp tee.

"But you *are* sweaty," she said in a breathy whisper.

Mark's mouth hovered over hers. "So are you."

Big brown eyes stared up at him igniting a fire in his soul. Something primitive and hot. Scorching hot. He brushed his lips over hers, and Ivy whimpered, saying in a heated whisper, "That makes us even."

The next thing Mark knew, his mouth was on hers, all hot and hungry, and Ivy was giving back as much as she was getting, molding her body up against his, sighing into his kisses. Mark thought he'd tasted passion before, but he'd been wrong. Nothing in his memory had set his soul ablaze like this, and other parts of his anatomy too.

When he pulled back, Ivy's cheeks glowed bright pink, and her eyes sparked with desire. "Do you have a thing about women in vehicles?"

"Only this woman," he said, kissing her again.

On the street beyond them, a car slowed, then drove past.

"We'd better cut it out," Ivy said before he could claim her mouth again. "You never know who's watching."

"Or who will be talking." Mark laughed and hugged her to him, giving her one more swift peck on the lips. "What time tomorrow?"

"Eight o'clock?"

Ivy was so dizzy from the taste of him, she missed the turn to her dirt road three times. The first time she skipped it, she excused herself for being distracted. The second time, she blamed it on the dark. By the time she wound up in the high school parking lot making her third U-turn, Ivy stopped and banged her head against the wheel. She had to get a grip! But all she could think of holding at the moment was one superhot Bostonian in her arms. He'd absolutely ravaged her with kisses.

Ivy was grateful she'd been sitting down, because she wasn't sure her knees could have stood up under the pressure.

She checked the time on her cell and saw she had less than an hour to clean up and meet Grace. They were doing a girls' night in honor of Caroline by surprising her with a wedding shower. While Ivy admitted it was a little awkward for her to be included, it would have looked more suspicious had she been left out, or worse—if she'd been invited but hadn't agreed to attend. As far as all of Rosemont was concerned, Ivy and Austin were history. Austin had moved on, and soon all would see that Ivy had too. She flushed from head to toe, thinking the townsfolk would assume Mark was her boyfriend. Then felt lead in the pit of her stomach when she realized that for her, at least, this was no longer a charade. The little plan she and Mark had concocted had somehow taken on a life of its own. The more they'd gotten to know each other, the more genuinely attracted to the other each of them had become.

It was impossible to deny it, especially after their time together on Saturday and this evening's scorching kisses. Ivy was falling for Mark, hook, line, and sinker, and she had every indication the feeling was mutual. But even it if was, what did that mean if Mark wasn't in Rosemont for the long haul? She'd asked him about his intentions of staying before, but he'd never given her a totally straight answer. Ivy pulled up to her cozy country cottage, her shoulders sagging with the realization. After all this time, she was finally opening herself up to someone. And that someone might just up and walk away. He might not run like Austin had, but if Mark left town to return to Boston after she'd become too deeply involved with him, the impact would be the same. Ivy didn't know if she was prepared to face that kind of hurt again. So maybe the best thing to do would be to put on the brakes and take things slow until she understood what Mark's future intentions were.

Mark pulled off his drenched tee and stepped into an extra-cold shower. *Brrrr*, but the water felt good. He badly needed to scrub off the grime, and the icy streams helped simmer down all that heat he'd built up kissing Ivy. There he'd gone and done it again! Gone and kissed her without planning it out or meaning to. No, that wasn't true. He'd meant to, all right. And he'd given her everything he had, full force. Mark rinsed off, then toweled dry, thinking he couldn't really blame himself for falling under Ivy's spell. She wasn't just pretty. She was smart and capable too. Just look at how she'd designed that landscaping project. And all on her own!

Mark wrapped the towel around his waist, then sauntered to the kitchen to grab a cold DelaStar draft. He popped it open, then stepped out onto his front porch to enjoy the cool of the evening. This was something he definitely couldn't do in Boston! There was a lot of privacy here. The nearest thing he had to neighbors were the cows in the adjoining field, and even they had gone in for the night. Mark watched as the sun tucked itself in behind the mountains, the sky taking on an orangey glow as day faded to night. There was a lot to like about Rosemont, he'd admit it. Especially one cute brunette with bangs who knew a thing or two about gardening. Mark took a long swig of beer, then studied the horizon, a new thought occurring. What if Ivy had an income stream to help pay for her beautification projects? One that wouldn't require a town fundraiser each and every time?

The wheels started turning in Mark's brain as he saw a bigger picture coming together. DelaStar Drafts made it a point to support the local economy. The company was big on charitable contributions and preserving green space as well. Mark snapped his fingers at the ease of the concept as it formed. Of course! One way that DelaStar could give back might be by contributing to projects like the one Ivy was undertaking at the library. They could earmark a special fund, maybe seek cooperative agreements with other entities like area nurseries and builder supply stores. Perhaps even fund an endowment to pay for regular employees to oversee and install this architectural landscaping. And it would all go to benefit public works: libraries, schools, parks, even fire stations! Mark was getting excited just at the thought. He hoped Ivy would find the idea enticing too. He'd run it by her tomorrow.

Chapter Fourteen

Ivy was a ball of nerves preparing for Mark. She didn't know why it was so much work to get the sauce right. She'd made Eustis's recipe dozens of times, and it always came out perfect. The balance didn't seem to be right with the herbs. Too much fresh basil, perhaps. Maybe she could disguise any culinary mistakes with a few extra shakes of parmesan cheese? She sure hoped Mark liked dairy. It was a warm evening, so Ivy had dressed casually in a wildflower-patterned sundress and strappy flat sandals. She wore a navy blue apron while cooking, both because she was in the habit of using one at the café and to protect her clothing from tomato sauce splatter.

She'd planned to have the table set and candles burning when Mark arrived, but the doorbell rang ten minutes early, sending Ivy racing into the powder room to check her reflection. Although her face was a bit glisteny from cooking over a hot stove and her hair had frizzed slightly, her makeup still looked okay. But oh! The apron. She quickly tugged it over her head, immediately noting black streaks down the back. *Mascara!* Ivy glanced in the mirror in horror to see she looked like a raccoon.

"Coming!" she called loudly when the doorbell rang again.

"Ivy?"

Oh no! It was Mark's voice, coming from inside the house. He must have heard her calling and let himself in through the screen door, since the main one was ajar.

Ivy stared at her reflection and made a quick call. She had no way to touch up in here, so it all had to come off. She ran the water and quickly scrubbed her face before patting it dry and throwing open the bathroom door, nearly hitting Mark in the chest.

"Whoa!" he cried, stepping back and holding his bottle of Chianti high. "There you are."

Ivy brought her hands to her flaming cheeks, thinking she probably didn't need rouge anyway. "Sorry, I was just—"

He peered through the open door at her back and saw it was a bathroom. "Gee, sorry," he said with a grimace. "I thought I heard you say *come in*."

Ivy laughed and waved her hand, hoping he wouldn't notice how plain she looked. Maybe once they'd served the wine, she could sneak upstairs and fix things. "It's all right," she told him, taking the bottle. "Good to see you made it here with my directions."

Mark looked around the comfortable but crowded room, which housed all sorts of memorabilia from famous gardens, and stacks upon stacks of landscaping books. Some cluttered the coffee table, while others formed piles on the floor. He was glad Ivy hadn't worried about picking up for him. That just proved how comfortable she felt in his presence. "Nice place."

"You should have seen it before I cleaned!" Ivy chirped lightly. "Please sit. I'll bring you something to open the wine."

"And a couple of goblets!" he called after her when she left the room.

Mark studied the sofa, trying to decide where to plant his derriere. There was an open newspaper on it with a picture of Walt on the front page! Wait. Was that a rear shot of Eustis? Something rattled under the paper, startling Mark back a step. Then a large calico cat stuck its head out from under the newspaper and yawned.

"I see you've met Orchid," Ivy said, returning. She handed Mark a corkscrew and slid two glasses onto the coffee table. Then she scooped up the newspapers and shooed the huge cat out of the way. It reluctantly circled a sofa cushion, then hopped down onto the floor to rub up against Mark's pant leg until he bent down to pet it. Orchid purred loudly, turning her pudgy face up to his.

"Hi, Orchid," he said, gently stroking the cat's head. "Nice to meet you."

The cat meowed in return, then sat on his foot.

"Looks like you have a friend," Ivy observed. "Hope you're not allergic."

"The only thing I can't tolerate is cheese," he said with a laugh.

Ivy's mouth fell open in apparent surprise. "You don't like it?"

"More like it doesn't like me." He sat on the sofa, and Orchid immediately jumped in his lap. Mark resigned himself to getting covered with cat hair and took to task uncorking the bottle as the weighty animal settled in. "But we're having spaghetti for dinner, right?"

"Right!" she said extra quickly. "No cheese! Not even parmesan."

"If you cook half as well as you garden, I know it will be outstanding."

Her cheeks flushed. "Thanks, Mark."

He opened the wine, then started to pour. "Should I let it breathe first?"

"It can breathe inside us."

Mark chuckled and filled her glass. "I like the way you think, Ivy."

She accepted her glass, then glanced toward the flight of wooden stairs. "If you'll excuse me a minute. I just remembered something I left...turned on."

"On?"

"Lights."

"Lights," Mark echoed, thinking it a shame Ivy fretted so much over her electric bill. He couldn't wait to tell her about his idea.

"It will just take a sec!" she said, dashing upstairs and splashing droplets of red wine as she went. Mark watched with amazement, then gingerly pushed the cat out of his lap before rising to tend to the hardwood steps. Some paper napkins sat on the coffee table. He'd nab a few to clean up Ivy's mess before she could realize it had happened.

He started at the bottom and nearly had all of them done when Ivy appeared on the landing. "Mark! What are you doing?"

He wadded up a napkin and shoved it in his pocket. "Just, um..."

"Were you actually sneaking up the stairs?" she asked, aghast.

"Sneaking? No!" He jumped back as the cat darted between his legs, nearly losing his footing. Mark clung to the rail and backed down one step at a time as Ivy approached. "I just..."

"What?" she asked, tilting her head to the side. It occurred to Mark that she looked extra pretty, even more gorgeous than she'd appeared when he'd arrived. Though he didn't know how that was possible. Orchid skirted behind her, then curled round her legs, following as she made her descent.

"Well, to tell you the truth," he said, his shoes finally hitting the carpet, "you spilled a little wine."

"I what?" Her brow rose, then she glanced down at the half-filled goblet in her hand. "Oh no." Then she shook her head and giggled. "I'm so sorry," she offered sincerely. "I guess I'm just a little keyed up tonight."

"Keyed up? But why?"

She shrugged as they sat together on the sofa. "I just wanted to make things perfect."

"But they *are* perfect. Can't you see?"

She hung her head with a blush. "You haven't even tasted my spaghetti yet."

"Doesn't matter. I still know I'll love it."

"There you go," she said with a sigh. "Doing it again."

"Doing what?"

"Being nice to me."

He met her eyes. "Is that some kind of crime in this precinct?"

Ivy laughed, her tension apparently easing. "No, but it makes things awfully difficult."

"Difficult how?" he asked.

"You make it pretty darn hard not to like you."

"Sweetheart," he said, toasting her glass, "the feeling is mutual."

"Mark…"

"Which is why I want to tell you about my plan," he said, barreling ahead.

"What plan?"

"DelaStar Drafts' latest endeavor. Charitable endeavor, that is. I hope that you'll approve and maybe even agree to be a part of it."

Ivy listened with interest as Mark mapped out his ideas. He was such a brilliant man, and always thinking of ways to improve things. And what a boon to Rosemont his proposed endowment could be. Ivy had often thought of places that needed improving, like the rundown courtyard in the retirement home near the edge of town. But her dreams had always run deeper than her pocketbook. When she was a teen, she used to tell Austin she hoped to change this place. Make it better for everyone here, maybe even an attraction for others stopping through. He'd practically scoffed at her and said, *"Yeah, right. Like who'd want to come to Rosemont?"*

Now, Mark was telling her the possibilities were endless. With his plant pumping money into the economy, capital would arise for new start-ups. People with existing businesses could improve them, just as he hoped Ivy would help develop the physical layout of the town, giving it a charming village feel. That would draw others to Rosemont, like prospective bed-and-breakfast owners looking to take one of the neglected old mansions and convert it to someplace spectacular where visitors could stay. Almost as a vacation destination of its own. Ivy's blood pumped faster as Mark described the possibilities.

"So, how exactly would it work?" she asked. "This endowment?"

"The company would donate a certain amount of money to establish the fund," he explained. "That fund would be the capital that earns interest. That interest would be used to pay for the kinds of improvements you're talking about, and finance a paid position or two to oversee that initiative's goals."

Ivy stared at him, intrigued. "A single fund could do all that?"

Mark grinned. "If it's large enough."

"Whoa."

"Listen, Ivy. Nothing's been worked out yet. There are people I'll need to talk to, shareholders and investors, so I don't want you to get your hopes up."

Her face fell, and he raised his glass.

"But you can be cautiously optimistic. That is, if you think it's the sort of thing you'd like to take on?"

"Would I?" She gave a happy gasp. "Getting to use my landscaping skills, help this town…and get paid for it too? That's like a dream come true."

He smiled warmly. "I'm glad to hear you say that. I'll look into it, then. And let you know what comes."

"Thank you. You really are a terrific guy."

"Anyone could have thought of it."

"I doubt that."

Mark's temples colored slightly. As great as he was, he clearly wasn't used to getting compliments. "Is there something I can do to help with dinner?"

"Dinner! Oh my gosh, I nearly forgot!" She shot a gaze at the clock, embarrassed. It was already past nine o'clock. "I honestly didn't mean to starve you."

"Not your fault," he said, standing to help her. "I was the one running off at the mouth."

"No. What you were saying was important. Way important. Such a great idea, Mark!" She kissed him on the cheek without warning, and the warmth of her lips tingled, reminding Mark of her sultry kisses in the truck. He caught her by the elbow before she could turn.

"I want to thank *you*, Ivy. For helping me see Rosemont in a different way. By letting me get to know the people and better understand the town."

"It's a great town," she told him. "A lot of people spend their lives here."

He met her eyes, and his gaze lingered. "I know what you're thinking. You're worried about whether or not I'll stay."

"I never said that."

"Maybe you didn't have to."

"Look, Mark. I'm a big girl now. I understand the sort of business you're in, because you've told me. You set up a new factory and then leave the town. Isn't that how it is?"

"Generally, yes."

"Then I'm under no illusions." But even as she said it, there was hurt in her voice.

He cupped her chin in his hand and spoke the only truth he could. "I can't make you any promises, because I just don't know."

Ivy straightened her spine. "Nobody asked you to."

"Apart from looking into the endowment, I mean. That's going to happen, one way or another."

One way or another, meaning whether or not Mark decided to break Ivy's heart, she thought with remorse. This wasn't boyfriend talk, or an indication Mark thought they might ultimately have a future together. He was prepping her for the letdown and trying to soften the blow by extending a very generous business offer. An offer Mark knew Ivy would find impossible to refuse. Ivy was right to think earlier she needed to proceed with caution. In fact, it would be better for her to stop proceeding at all. Falling back into Mark's arms

screen door, sobs racking her body. Then she fell onto
the sofa and curled up in a ball. She didn't know when
Orchid joined her, but sometime in the night she
reached out and found the feline snuggled up at her
side. It was the only comfort she had, and maybe all
that she deserved, Ivy thought, crying herself back to
sleep. Who was she to think that Mark might come here
and change his whole life just for her? She'd been even
more delusional now than she'd been with Austin.
Hadn't she learned her lessons by now?

Ivy drifted off fitfully, trying not to remember the
good times with Mark, but they pelted her
consciousness anyway. Yet the picture that was clearest
was the look of disdain in Mark's eyes as he'd turned
and walked away. Ivy had blown things, all right.
Blown them big-time.

Mark tossed and turned in bed, unable to sleep
soundly. He sure wasn't looking forward to that
wedding with Ivy, but he'd said he would take her, so
he was going to. It was hard to understand how things
had turned bad so quickly. They'd been getting along
great and obviously shared some sort of chemistry.
Mark frowned hard, remembering that *chemistry* wasn't
everything. Just look where it had landed him with
Sandra.

He fluffed his pillow and shoved his arm beneath
it, settling his head back down on top. And to think—
just yesterday—he and Ivy had shared that sexy kiss in
her truck. Well, there'd apparently be no more kissing
with her, or any other sort of involvement. And that was
fine with him. Extra good. Just dandy. He clearly didn't
need to get caught up with some woman in Rosemont
when his life plans were taking him elsewhere.

Mark grumbled to himself that life's plans weren't always what they were cracked up to be. Though there was one plan Mark was determined to ensure: the endowment for Rosemont's beautification fund. The more he thought about the idea, the more he liked it. Ivy was right on that score. The concept was a winner. And not just for Rosemont either. Mark hoped to implement something similar in all his DelaStar Drafts towns. He'd start looking into it tomorrow. His focus on that and getting the factory going would keep him busy the rest of this week. Then he'd just have to get through Saturday.

After that, he'd be a free man. Free to return to Boston and move on with his life, without some sweet Southern woman casting aspersions on his character. Mark was done with judgmental women. Past done. After Austin's wedding was over, he was going to prove it.

Chapter Fifteen

Eustis arrived at four on Saturday to start getting ready at Ivy's house. She'd said she wanted Ivy's help with her hair, but Ivy suspected she mainly wanted company. Eustis was nervous as a cat on a hot tin roof about her big date with Walt. Ivy wasn't sure why, since they'd already gone out for tea and dinner. Perhaps it was because this seemed a bigger step, more formal. Plus Eustis and Walt would be appearing as a couple for the first time before the town. That was, if you didn't count the story in the paper.

Ivy held back the screen door as Eustis sashayed inside, carting a pretty green dress in a cleaner's bag. She clutched a pair of matching shoes in her other hand, and a portable makeup bag hung from a strap over her shoulder. Her short auburn hair was in clips tightly pinching each damp curl to hold it in place. "I thought I'd go natural. What do you think?" she asked Ivy, noting the other's gaze on her hair.

Ivy knew natural meant curly to Eustis. Her real hair was stick straight, but Eustis permed it. "Want me to help set it?"

Eustis hung her dress from a doorframe, then produced a tin of Creamy Curls from her bag. "Would you?" she asked with a grin.

"Of course, come on in," she said, shutting the wooden door at Eustis's back. "We're letting out the air-conditioning."

"Best to stay cool while we can," Eustis replied in a singsongy voice. "We're going out with two hot men!"

Normally, Ivy would have laughed, but today her spirits were low. She'd been glum ever since her Tuesday night dinner with Mark, but had hidden her feelings from Eustis. Eustis had been super bubbly all week, glowing like a tree lit up at Christmas each time Walt had looked her way. And he'd been looking plenty. Ivy'd been watching and didn't believe he'd finished an entire crossword puzzle all week. Mostly, he appeared to be mooning over Eustis. That, and daydreaming some.

"What are you wearing?" Eustis asked, noting Ivy was still in the robe she'd slipped into after her shower.

"The powder-blue dress."

"Ooh, the short one with spaghetti straps?"

Ivy nodded. "Can I get you something cold to drink? Maybe iced tea?"

"Got any white wine?" Eustis asked with a grin.

A little while later, they were busy upstairs getting ready. Ivy had just finished Eustis's hair, and stood behind her now as Eustis studied her reflection in the mirror. "Nice," the older woman said. "Now if you could just take ten years off my face, we'd be in business. Oh," she said, lifting the hem of her dress, "and can you do something about the cellulite too?"

"Shush!" Ivy patted her shoulders, admiring her friend. "You look gorgeous, and you know it."

Eustis peered over her shoulder to meet Ivy's eyes. "Do you really think Walt will think so?"

"Walt's going to pass out. And I don't mean from the summer heat."

Eustis laughed lightly and picked up her wine. "Are you feeling all right, Ivy?"

Ivy noticed Eustis's gaze on her glass and picked it up. "Sure, why?"

"I don't know. You seem a little…down? Not nearly as excited as I thought you'd be."

Ivy took a swig of wine, then spoke quickly. "It's just an arrangement Eustis. Not a real date."

"But I thought you and Mark *were* dating. Didn't you go to lunch, then out for ice cream, *and* out to the swimming hole later?"

"We were getting to know each other, yeah."

"Well, if that's what you call making out in public, then—"

"Making out?" Ivy asked with a gasp. "Whatever do you mean?"

"Myrtle Wilcox saw the two of you."

"Myrtle Wilcox?" Ivy echoed in shock. Ivy knew that Myrtle worked in the town pharmacy but was most practiced in dispensing gossip. "When?"

"Monday evening outside the library. Said you and Mark were engaged in a lip-lock that could set Rosemont ablaze. She nearly called the fire department."

Ivy sat heavily on the bed and held her wine. "Wonderful."

Eustis studied her with concern. "It sounded pretty good to me."

Ivy hung her head and surveyed her toenails through her strappy black sandals. She'd painted them pomegranate red to match her lipstick, but now she didn't feel much like putting that on.

"What's going on, hon?" Eustis asked softly.

"It's Mark," Ivy said, her voice trembling. "He's going away."

"He said that?"

Ivy looked up. "Didn't have to. It's what he's always done. Run out."

"Sounds like you're confusing him with Austin."

"Well, maybe Mark *is* like Austin in one very important way."

"Oh? What's that?"

Ivy pursed her lips as tears leaked from her eyes. "He made me fall in love with him, and now he's leaving."

"In...?" Eustis took Ivy's wine and set it aside with her own, then sat down on the bed to hug her. "Oh my sweet, baby. You did?"

Ivy met her gaze and nodded.

"That's wonder—" Eustis started before noting Ivy's expression and quickly backtracking. "Terrible! Horrible. The most tragic thing on earth. Poor child." She wrapped her arms around Ivy and pulled her close while Ivy wept. "Love is a vicious thing."

After a moment, Eustis grabbed a tissue from the nightstand and handed it to her. "You don't have to go to the wedding if you're not feeling up to it. I'll tell folks you got a headache, came down with the flu. Something like that."

Ivy dabbed her eyes and balled up the tissue, seeing it was black with mascara. Great. She'd have to start over. "No. I'm going."

Eustis's face was etched with concern. "Are you sure?"

"I need to, Eustis. For myself, and to show them."

"Show whom, sweetie?"

"Both Austin and Mark that I'm not afraid. I can handle this, you know. I'm not the same person I was six years ago. I'm stronger."

Walt arrived first, looking dapper in a three-piece suit and bowtie. "Why, Walt Winters," Eustis proclaimed, throwing open the door. "You look dashing!"

"Yes, he does," Ivy agreed. She'd never seen Walt so prettied up. It even looked like he'd whitened his teeth!

"And you ladies look lovely. It's going to be hard for folks to focus on the bride when you two walk in."

Eustis blushed and picked up her clutch. "You do have a way with words, Mr. Winters."

"I'm terribly proud to be taking you," Walt told Eustis. "Thanks for saying yes."

She met his gaze, and her eyes sparkled. "Thanks for asking me."

Ivy bid them good-bye after they agreed to meet up later. Walt and Eustis would save seats for her and Mark in the church, then they'd all get a table together at the reception. Grace and her husband would join them there too. Ivy watched the happy couple stride down the walk toward Walt's high-end car. Walt offered Eustis an arm, and she leaned into him, giggling with delight as he likely shared some further compliments.

"You kids have fun!" Ivy called from the porch before heading back indoors.

Mark arrived a few minutes later, and Ivy was ready. As soon as she saw his SUV through the window, she stepped onto the porch, as she wasn't interested in having him come inside. It was likely more comfortable for him this way as well, Ivy thought, striding toward the drive. Mark stepped from his vehicle and walked to meet her, stopping her halfway down the path. "Wow, Ivy," he said, admiring her outfit. "You look beautiful." She'd put up her hair in a French twist and had uncharacteristically swept her bangs to the side. Long sparkly earrings dangled from her earlobes, and a pretty heart necklace hung from a skinny silver chain around her neck.

She took in Mark's tailored charcoal suit, his red-striped tie, and the pressed blue shirt that matched his eyes, admitting to herself that he looked dynamite as well. "You're not so bad yourself," she told him. "Should we get going?"

"Is Eustis...?" he began before she cut in.

"Walt picked her up a few minutes ago."

"Good. Then we're meeting them there?"

"They're saving seats for us."

Mark opened the passenger-side door, and Ivy climbed in, feeling polished and cool for the first time. She could do this, *she could*. Plus, she'd worn her lucky necklace for good measure.

Once Mark had buckled up, he eyed Ivy fastening her seat belt. "That's a very pretty charm," he said, indicating the delicate silver heart that dipped toward her cleavage.

"Thanks. It was a gift," she answered, leading him to believe it might have been a present from some guy. The truth was, Ivy had given it to herself. She'd purchased it as a graduation reward shortly after earning her degree. She'd viewed it as celebratory on two counts. First, because she'd managed to put herself through college, which had been no small financial feat. And second, because she'd decided that, even if she never found a man to love her, it wouldn't so much matter as long as Ivy loved herself. The necklace was special in many ways, but one of the most important was as a mark of her independence. Which was why she had purposely chosen to wear it today.

"I had some good news this week," Mark told her as they headed toward town. "About the endowment."

Ivy was tempted to bubble over with excitement, but then refocused on her cloudy emotions concerning Mark. It was hard to get too enthused about his proposition with her personal feelings caught up in the mix. Then again, Ivy was decidedly curious about the outcome. Particularly since it could benefit Rosemont. "Oh?"

He turned to her briefly and grinned. "The board members loved it. The shareholders too. Everyone's behind the idea of a Rosemont Beautification Fund. In fact, they want to establish one in every DelaStar Drafts location."

"Well. That's fantastic," she said, unable to deny that it was. What a terrific boon this would be for Rosemont! And not just during the immediate future, but long-term. Revamping the physical aspects of the community truly could have a positive impact, just as Mark had implied.

"Some people will be driving down in a few weeks to meet with local authorities and talk about it."

"You mean the mayor?"

"Yeah, and the fire chief. Hopefully some members from the school board and from public works. I was kind of hoping that you might be there too. That is, if you still want to be involved in helming the project." It was too good an opportunity to pass up, for both Ivy and the town.

"Will you be there?" she asked him.

Mark shook his head. "Not at that meeting. I've got other people assigned to oversee charitable operations.

You'll like them, though. Everyone's really easy to get along with, and all have the right goals in mind."

"Helping other people."

"Exactly."

Ivy studied his handsome profile, thinking once again what an accomplished man he was. He'd surprised her with his demeanor too. After their last parting, Ivy had been a little worried that Mark might act cold upon seeing her again. Fortunately, he didn't appear to be the sort to hold grudges. Still, Ivy had been rather rude in what she'd said about Sandra and felt driven to apologize. "Mark, about the other night."

"Water under the bridge," he told her.

"No, really—"

"Ivy," he said, stopping her, "let's just set that aside." He took his eyes off the road for a second to glance at her. "I mean it."

"If that's what you want."

Mark gripped the wheel. "What I want is for us to get through today just as we planned. I'm as sorry as you are that things didn't go smoothly between us on Tuesday. Maybe more." He drew a breath, then released it. "Here's the thing. Neither of us intended to get involved, but somehow we did. Now, stepping back and looking forward, we can probably both see that was a mistake."

"I certainly think so," Ivy lied.

He pursed his lips and stared out the windshield for an extended beat before saying hoarsely, "Me too."

She blinked and turned away. "Then we're agreed. We get through the wedding, then say good-bye."

"I think that's for the best, don't you?"

Ivy didn't see how it could be any other way. Not now that she knew how Mark really felt about her. Or rather, how he *didn't.* "And about the Beautification Fund?"

"I won't be directly involved, just like I said. But I still want to do this for Rosemont. It's a good thing. The right thing."

And you always do the right thing, don't you? Ivy wanted to say. But this time she held her tongue.

"The truth is," he said, "I have meetings scheduled in Boston on Monday. I'm already packed and plan to leave in the morning."

Ivy steeled her heart, then spoke with a shaky smile.

"Then, I'll wish you safe travels."

Chapter Sixteen

Mark escorted Ivy up the stone steps to the church, an uncanny déjà vu taking hold. Good thing they were entering through the front doors and not near the chancel. Mark got itchy-footed just thinking about it. Not that he'd ever be inclined to run again. Mark had learned a hard lesson with Sandra, and that lesson was you should never plan to marry a woman when your heart wasn't sure. If Mark had been honest with himself rather than allowing Sandra to reason him into it, he never would have purchased that engagement ring. Mark adjusted his jacket and shook off the feeling, wondering if Ivy was growing uncomfortable too. She and churches had the same sort of tangled history. "How you doing?" he whispered, leaning toward her.

She looked beautiful this evening, with her dark hair piled up and those dangly earrings sparkling against the line of her neck. Maybe even more beautiful than he'd ever seen her. "Okay. How about you?"

Mark heard organ music ahead. Then… *Oh no. Not that.* The first five chords of "Ave Maria." Mark broke into a sweat, moisture sweeping his hairline and warming the back of his neck. His jaw tightened. "I'm good. Extra good."

Ivy eyed him curiously and lifted an eyebrow. "You sure?" she whispered back.

Mark nodded and stepped through the huge oaken door into the hull of the church, following Ivy. She withdrew a tissue from her purse and handed it to him so he could wipe his brow, then accepted two printed programs from a flower girl distributing them with a smile.

"I think I see Eustis," she said, peering through the door to the sanctuary.

Good, Mark thought, they were seated near the back. That could prove handy if he felt the need to make a quick exit. All of a sudden, he felt sick to his stomach.

Ivy studied his face with concern. "You're not looking so well."

He forced a smile. "I'll be all right. As soon as I sit down."

Walt and Eustis scooted over in the pew, making room. Mark let Ivy sit first beside Eustis, then took his seat near the aisle, feeling foolish. Here he was, with his stomach in knots, when the one who really had call to be nervous was Ivy. It was her ex-fiancé's wedding, after all. He glanced her way as the soprano started to sing, noting Ivy looked cool as a cucumber, poised and lovely, sitting upright in that short blue dress that showed off her legs and cutely colored toenails. Ivy caught him looking at her feet, and Mark felt even more overheated in his jacket than he had before.

"Drop something?" she asked him.

Mark casually let his program slip from his hand and onto the floor near the aisle. "Oh! There it is," he said quietly to her. "Sorry."

She narrowed her gaze, then whispered something to Eustis. So Mark decided to focus on the show. Ceremony. Whatever it was. Why did they always have to play that song? Mercifully, it ended, and a processional began. Mark checked his cell, seeing they were starting right on time. Groomsmen appeared near the chancel, the best man flanking Austin. Mark thought of Wayne and how out of touch they'd been since Mark's failed nuptials. He would definitely have to fill Wayne in. Maybe he'd call him up for a beer when he got back to Boston. So much had occurred since they'd spoken last. Wayne didn't even know about Ivy.

The first bridesmaid appeared just as a dead weight settled in Mark's stomach. Wayne didn't know about Ivy, because Mark hadn't wanted to tell him. He'd been afraid to spill about becoming involved again so soon after Sandra. Wayne might have found it hard to believe that Mark could like someone as much as he had Ivy. Mark had been taken aback by it himself. But the truth was, he'd been attracted to her from the very beginning. Once he'd gotten to know her, and had begun really putting Sandra behind, him, he'd fallen even harder. Rock hard. His heart still felt bruised by it.

More bridesmaids promenaded forward, and then the small girl who'd been handing out programs arrived to scatter rose petals down the aisle. The first bars of "Here Comes the Bride" played, and the wedding guests rose. Mark turned to see Caroline standing at the door to the sanctuary looking very pretty in her wedding gown. Then he glanced at Ivy beside him and had a vision of her dressed in white. With her dark hair and eyes and creamy complexion, Ivy must have made a stunning bride. Would make a stunning bride again. Some day, for the right man. Mark swallowed hard when he realized what he'd been thinking. He'd been imagining himself as the groom.

Ivy didn't think Mark looked all that well. He'd literally broken into a sweat the moment they'd stepped onto sacred grounds. Maybe this was too much too soon for him, coming to another church wedding only a few months after being jilted at his own. No, wait. It was

Mark who'd done the jilting. Or did Ivy have it wrong, and was it the other way around?

She tried to put herself in Mark's place when he'd discovered Sandra's infidelity only minutes before he was supposed to wed her. Not only that, Sandra was a serial cheater, or at the very least a repeat offender. Mark had told Ivy about it at the swimming hole, including that bit about how he'd found Sandra making out with Frank back at his house on his very own sofa. Talk about adding insult to injury! No wonder Mark had been incensed. And devastated, Ivy thought, casting him a sideways glance.

He looked incredibly gorgeous standing there in his suit and tie, even if he did appear uncomfortable. With the whole town packed in, the temperature was rising in here due to sheer body heat alone, never mind the ninety-degree temperatures outdoors. Ivy felt grateful she was a woman and could wear a skimpy spaghetti-strap dress. Mark, in the meantime, had to suffer in layered-up silence.

Caroline joined Austin at the altar, and the preacher motioned for the wedding guests to sit. After Caroline's parents gave her away, the exchange of vows began in earnest. Eustis sniffled, and Walt took her hand, holding it sweetly in his while patting it with his other. Ivy pried open her purse and pulled out more tissues, handing some to Eustis. She was glad she'd brought the extra pack, thinking she might shed a tear or two herself. Instead, she sat here dry eyed, doling out comfort to Eustis and…Mark, who was still sweating. She handed him a few more, and he took them with a grateful nod.

This was almost surreal. Austin was getting married! Her Austin. No, not her Austin, Ivy reminded

herself. He was Caroline's now. Poor woman. Ivy
stifled a giggle, surprised at herself. She wasn't
supposed to be thinking those things, but she was.
Pitying the bride in question. Suddenly, it all came back
to her. The way Austin ate like a caveman and talked
with his mouth full. How he was even messier than she
was, and left his smelly socks everywhere. *What did he
have? Some kind of foot fungus?* The way he played
electric bass to all hours and sang off key, because he
had ambitions of becoming a Nashville country star.
That he was allergic to cats. And trees. And grass! And
who knew what else? A tear escaped her, but it wasn't
because of Austin. It was for Caroline.

Mark misunderstood, patting her arm.

Ivy thought it was sweet of him to care and try to
offer her comfort, especially given the awkward
situation they were in. But she didn't need Mark's
comfort, or anyone else's for that matter. Ivy
understood more fully now than ever that she could
take care of herself. When the ceremony ended and the
recessional started, Ivy sighed with relief.

Mark eyed her with compassion. "I'm really sorry
you had to see that," he said under his breath.

"Yeah," Eustis quipped quietly from the other side.
"Must have been hard."

"Not as much as it will be," Ivy whispered back.
"On Caroline."

Eustis, Mark, and Walt stared at her.

But instead of offering anything further, Ivy just sat
up a little straighter, her lips curved in a grin.
Empowerment felt good. Better than good.
Outstanding. So did making a narrow escape. Didn't
matter that it had happened years before. The same fact
remained. Ivy had gotten off the hook from marrying

Austin. And, in a strange way, he'd done her a favor. A favor she'd never felt more like celebrating than today.

The reception was held at a nearby vineyard at nightfall. Shadows from the darkening mountains stretched long, working their way toward an enormous patio flanked by flickering torches. It held a dance floor at one end and a hot hors d'oeuvres buffet at the other, with a smattering of tables with linen tablecloths in between.

"Wow," Mark said, approaching. "This is quite a spread."

"Caroline's family is well set," Eustis whispered to him.

"Means they're loaded," Walt explained.

Mark noticed that the older lovebirds were holding hands as they stepped into the lead, walking happily toward the celebration. If Ivy had brought Mark here to pose as her boyfriend, it sure didn't seem like it. She'd been distant ever since their conversation on the way to the wedding. Maybe Mark shouldn't have dumped all his plans on her then, including his intentions to leave Rosemont. Though it wasn't like she'd seemed opposed. In fact, she'd sounded glad to see him go. Heat flashed to his belly as his gut clenched. He hoped he wasn't coming down with something. Then he glanced at Ivy and realized he already had. She was radiant in that formfitting dress that accentuated her excellent figure, and her hairstyle made her look very sophisticated. He'd almost swear she'd stepped out of a charity gala in Boston. But he knew better. Ivy was nothing like those women. She was genuine and sincere.

Music played from a live band as the scent of summer lilacs filled the air. Candles flickered in the center of tables set for six. "Want to get something to drink?" Mark asked Ivy, "or should we find a table first?"

"We'd probably better find a place to sit." Then her eyes lit up and her smile brightened as she waved to a couple across the patio. "Looks like Grace and Donald already have."

The petite blonde and the stocky dark-haired guy with a marine's cut motioned them over to their table near the edge of the patio. "We saved places for you guys," the woman said. She smiled at Mark. "I'm Grace."

He nodded, then shook Donald's hand, who also introduced himself. "Mark Delacroix."

"Nice to finally meet you in person," Grace said.

"We've talked quite a bit on the phone," Mark explained to her husband.

"Hi, Eustis!" Grace said.

Donald extended his grip toward the older man. "Walt."

Everyone exchanged pleasantries as the group settled in.

"Delacroix…" Donald replied thoughtfully. "You're that new guy, right? The one with the microbrew?"

"That's me!"

Grace appeared sheepish. "I'm sorry I picked on you so badly in the beginning," she said.

"It's all right," Mark answered congenially. "You've made up for it."

"Well, you haven't quite made up for it with me and Walt!" Eustis said, pretending to act haughty. "We didn't even *know* you were going to run that proposal piece."

Grace's cheeks bloomed bright pink. "Well, Eustis... Walt..." She cautiously eyed them both. "It *was* news."

"And everyone loves some good news," Donald defended her. "Every once in a while."

Eustis adjusted her wrap. "You still might have told me. I am your auntie after all."

From what Ivy had told Mark, he knew they weren't blood related, but surmised Eustis had formed a family-type bond with Grace just as she had with Ivy after Ivy's parents were gone.

"Come on, Eustis," Grace pleaded. "Don't be mad. Isn't there something I can say?"

"No." The older woman pouted. "But there's something you can do."

Walt sat there tight-lipped, obviously content to let Eustis handle things.

Grace stared at Eustis expectantly, and Eustis pointed across the patio.

"Bring us some of that bubbly over there."

Mark glanced that way to spy waiters carting heavy trays through the crowd and distributing champagne flutes to the guests. When he turned back to Eustis, he was surprised to see her lips twitching in a grin. "Pretty please?" she asked sweetly.

"Why, Aunt Eustis!" Grace cried, laughing. "I seriously thought you were mad at me!"

Eustis giggled, then exchanged glances with Walt. "Naw, baby. Nobody's angry."

Walt wrapped his arm around her shoulders. "Seems you gave us quite a bit of publicity. People have been asking for our autographs."

Grace's mouth hung open. "Really?"

This was news to Mark, but apparently not Ivy, who supplied another detail. "They're asking them to sign the newspaper."

"Well, that's…awesome!" Grace eyed both Eustis and Walt. "I think?"

Walt chuckled warmly and held Eustis more tightly. "I don't mind being a celebrity if she doesn't."

Eustis beamed up at him. "Your pic was more flattering than mine."

"Not in my estimation," he said sweetly.

Ivy pulled the wedding program from her purse and fanned her face. "Lots of sugar being served at this table."

Grace's gaze panned over Ivy and the handsome man at her side. "Uh-huh." She stood, and Donald joined her. "I'm going to grab some of that bubbly."

"I'll help," he said. "We'll bring some back for everybody."

Ivy smiled at them both. "Sounds great! Thanks."

When Grace and Donald left in search of champagne, Eustis said, "I think I'll run and powder my nose before they get back."

"I'll come with you," Walt said.

"Why, Walt!" Eustis teased with a sassy edge. "You're not allowed in the ladies'."

He chuckled, then helped her with her chair. "I'll wait outside."

Since Eustis and Walt had ridden here with them from the church, this was the first time Mark and Ivy had been alone. Mark used the opportunity to delicately broach the subject. "I'm sorry if you're mad at me," he said, meaning it absolutely. The more the evening wore on, the more Mark was sensing he was making a mess of it. And the reception was just getting started.

Ivy turned pretty brown eyes on his. Color lightly dusted her cheeks. "Who says I'm mad?"

"You've hardly said two words to me since the ceremony."

"I've had a lot on my mind."

"I'm sure that was tough, seeing Austin—"

"No," she answered firmly. "That part was good. What I mean is, I'm okay with Caroline and Austin." She met his gaze with a soft smile. "In many ways, I'm glad it was her and not me."

Mark lowered his voice and leaned forward. "Sort of like you dodged a bullet, you mean?" he asked, knowing exactly what that felt like.

"Yeah."

"That's what I thought about Sandra."

"Sometimes things don't work out for a reason." When she said it, it was almost like she was talking about the two of them, and not their relationships with their exes.

"Ivy, about us…" He laid a hand on hers, which rested on the table, but she withdrew it.

"You really don't need to go there. I pretty much know where we stand."

"Why aren't you two dancing?" Grace asked, returning with a nest of glasses.

Donald carried more. He nodded toward the band. "Dance floor's already flooded."

Mark looked that way, seeing it was true. The wedding party was still at the church taking photos. It would be a while before they arrived to form a receiving line. Apparently, the guests had decided to make the best of the lull by kicking up their heels.

"It's okay," Donald whispered to them. "We won't let any cats out of the bag."

"Cats?" Mark asked.

"We know you're trying to keep it a secret," Grace said confidentially. "But everyone can tell you two are together."

"What?" Ivy asked.

"Come on, Ivy. We saw that eye-lock you two were engaged in just now. Honestly, I don't know why you haven't gone public about it."

"Plus…" Donald leaned forward and spoke in a mischievous tone, "Myrtle Wilcox saw you down at the library."

Ivy's eyes widened.

"If you're trying to keep things quiet out of sensitivity to Austin," Grace started, "I don't think you need to worry."

Donald agreed. "I think it's safe to say he's moved on."

Ivy stood suddenly, her knees knocking the table and sending champagne sloshing.

"Where are you going?" Mark asked.

"Over"—she pointed to the dance floor—"there!"

Mark chased after her, passing Eustis and Walt returning to the table on the way.

"What's going on?" Eustis asked.

"Dancing!" Mark replied, picking up his pace.

Over his shoulder, Mark heard her whisper to Walt, "I told you they were going to make it."

Chapter Seventeen

Ivy barreled onto the dance floor, her head and heart reeling. Music crescendoed and bodies twirled around her in a vivid display, swirling sequined dresses catching the torches' glow. She'd been fine all evening. So pulled together. Until now. "Ivy?" She felt a hand on her shoulder and turned to find Mark standing there, his face registering concern. "What's going on?"

Ivy couldn't tell him the truth. She'd only just figured it out herself. Ever since Tuesday, she'd been getting used to the idea that Mark was leaving. Heading back to Boston as soon as he could. Then earlier tonight, he'd confirmed it. It wasn't until Ivy realized the town was already seeing them as a couple that she fell apart. The irony didn't escape her that this was precisely what she'd wanted. Only when she and Mark had first concocted their plan, she'd had no clue how hard the evening would be.

The music stopped, and a slower song began. Some couples left the dance floor, while others paired up, swaying gently together. People started to notice Mark and Ivy standing in the midst of them but not dancing. Heads swiveled their way, and a few folks exchanged whispers. Mark was devastatingly gorgeous in his charcoal suit and tie, his blue shirt picking up the color of his eyes. They crinkled slightly at the corners. He held out his hands. "Maybe we should dance?"

Ivy had the instinct to run, but instead she stepped forward and into Mark's arms. He settled one hand at her waist and lifted his palm to hers on the other side. "It doesn't matter what people think," he whispered to her. "Or what they say." His fingers slid through hers, lacing their raised hands together. "All that matters is this dance."

He pulled her to him then, and guided her expertly around the dance floor in fluid strides. Ivy melted in his arms. She wanted to stay strong and guard her heart against him, but she felt herself getting swept away. "Where did you learn to dance like this?"

"I've never danced before," Mark lied.

Or maybe that was true, because instead of dancing, it felt like they were flying, soaring like birds in the sky. Mark's hand slipped from her waist to her lower back as he spun her around again. Ivy gasped, but he held her tighter, letting her know he was in command. She'd never been with a man so sure of his moves, or so completely in control of his body. It made her yearn to surrender and let him take control of hers. The music stopped, and Mark looked down, still holding her in his arms. They stood torso to torso, heart to beating heart. "You're beautiful."

"So are you." He lowered his head and Ivy's pulse quickened.

They were lost in the heat of the moment. Oblivious to others around them.

Blue eyes sparkled. "I need to kiss you."

Ivy held her breath as his mouth closed in.

"Say yes."

Ivy's heart beat wildly. She didn't care about tomorrow or the next day. There was just one thing she wanted—right now. Ivy tilted up her chin and whispered, "Yes."

She accepted his kiss like a woman standing under a waterfall. It poured down and into her, drenching her in its sweetness. The next thing she knew, Ivy heard hoots and hollers. Then whistles and clapping. She and

Mark broke apart to see the stunned wedding party had arrived.

Austin stood there, his jaw unhinged. "Ivy?"

Mark met her gaze with a wink before firmly taking her hand. Then he led her through the murmuring masses and straight up to the newlywed couple. Mark dipped his head at Caroline, then offered to shake Austin's hand. "Let us be among the first," he said, pulling Ivy up beside him, "to offer our congratulations to the happy couple."

"Sweet cherry pie!" Eustis exclaimed at their table. "You, honey," she said to Mark, "handled that just right."

Mark agreed with her about the move concerning Austin. But what about him putting the moves on Ivy on the dance floor? He hadn't intended to do it, but when she'd molded up against him, all warm and womanly in his arms, he'd almost felt as if he'd had no choice. His heart had given him no choice. It kept telling him over and over again, *don't let Ivy get away.*

Ivy blushed brilliantly and took a sip of champagne. "Guess that cat's out of the bag now," she said more to Donald than the others.

"Well, I think it's fine!" Grace proclaimed. "That's what weddings are for. Making merry."

Donald took her hand. "Speaking of which…" He gave her a sultry look. "It's getting late."

"What?"

Donald lifted an eyebrow, and Grace blushed. "Right!" she said, getting it. "We've got to relieve the babysitter. Plus…" She staged a yawn. "Both of us have had really long days."

"Bet they're aiming for an even longer night," Eustis whispered to Walt a little too loudly.

Walt chuckled, then cleared his throat. "Yes, well. Don't let us keep you. In fact…" He checked his watch. "It's nearly my bedtime too."

Eustis eyed him with disappointment before he surprised her with his next thought. "How about we get out of here?"

The reception had gone on for two hours and didn't show signs of slowing down. "But they haven't tossed the bouquet yet," Eustis said.

Mark feigned a cough to hide his grin. He met Ivy's eyes and knew she was thinking the same thing. Eustis was hoping to catch it. To the delight of them all, the maid of honor took the microphone from the bandleader and made an announcement.

"Perfect timing," Ivy told the others with a grin.

"Aren't you going to go?" Mark asked Ivy a few minutes later, once Caroline had appeared on the stage with her bouquet, and a group of interested ladies had gathered below it.

"I think I'll leave that to the other girls." The truth was, Ivy wasn't sure how much more excitement she could take in one night. That dance with Mark had completely undone her. And his kiss, *wow*. That had been a killer. It had been telling too, making Ivy wonder if Mark was really as bent on leaving Rosemont as he professed to be. So much had happened this past week that Ivy's head was spinning. It was hard to guess what would come next, so instead she decided to focus on the moment.

"Don't look at me," Grace said, thumbing her chest. "I'm married—*with kids*." She and Donald had decided to stay for the bouquet toss once they'd heard it was imminent. Eustis and Walt were hanging around too.

"Eustis?" Ivy urged. "Why aren't you down there?"

"Oh no... I..." the other woman demurred. "I think I'm a little old for that."

"You most certainly are not," Walt said, lifting her by the elbow.

She turned to him, surprised. "Walt?"

Dark eyes twinkled. "Break a leg, baby."

Eustis squealed when the bouquet landed in her hands. Of course, she'd nearly tackled three other ladies to get it, but no one at their table was going to mention that. Least of all Walt. He stood proudly beside her as they said their good-byes. Grace and Donald had offered to drive them back to the church, since it was on their way home. Mark had asked Ivy if she was ready to go, but she'd said no, she wanted to stay awhile. Mark was happy to keep her company as long as she wanted. In many ways, he hated for this evening to end.

The other four were walking away when a pair of giggling teenage girls ran up to Walt and Eustis, carrying a newspaper and a pen. "They weren't kidding about that?" Mark asked Ivy with surprise.

Eustis beamed and autographed the news story before Walt added his signature to the page as well.

"Nope," Ivy said with a smile. "They're town celebrities, all right."

"Maybe it doesn't take much in Rosemont."

"What do you mean?"

"Apparently I was one once too."

"Yeah, that's true." Ivy fiddled with stem of her champagne flute before meeting his gaze. "That was some kiss on the dance floor."

"My feelings exactly."

"Nearly blew my socks off."

Mark glanced under the table, then met her eyes. "You're not wearing any socks."

Her cheeks reddened. "Heels, then."

Mark sighed with sweet recollection and leaned back in his chair. "I know exactly what you're saying. We're good together like that."

Ivy studied him. "I suppose chemistry's not everything."

Mark wondered if this was a trick question, and whether he was going to get ambushed one way or another, no matter what he said. So instead he just offered, "Hmm."

"What's *hmm*?" she challenged, apparently not willing to let him off the hook that easily.

"Some folks say it's not. But, at the end of the day, it certainly doesn't hurt."

"All other things being equal."

"Yes."

"Like mutual trust and affection."

"And respect." Mark held up his hand. "It's important for people in a"—he paused on the word—"relationship to respect each other."

"I'll drink to that."

Ivy raised her glass, and he clinked it.

They stared out at the crowd, which was dispersing as the waitstaff began clearing empty tables.

"It's a damn shame you don't live in Boston," he said after a beat.

"It's a damn shame you're leaving Rosemont," she returned.

Mark met Ivy's gaze and held it. "Ever consider moving?"

"Ever consider staying?"

"You didn't answer my question."

"I'm not a big-city kind of girl."

"Well, maybe I'm not a small-town guy."

She twisted her lips and stared at him. "No, maybe you're not."

Then, after a few more minutes of silence, they decided to go.

The next morning, Mark tossed the last of his bags in his SUV with a heavy heart. He knew he shouldn't beat himself up over Rosemont. He'd accomplished what he'd set out to do, and then some. The factory was up and running, and he'd started a number of local initiatives besides. The Beautification Fund was just the latest idea, and he would always be grateful to Ivy for providing the inspiration for him thinking it up.

Mark drove down his pebbled drive with a parting glance at the mountains and the herd of cattle across the way. He was leaving Rosemont a better place than he'd found it. But if Mark was so proud of his achievements, why was he feeling down? It was likely because of his mixed-up feelings concerning Ivy. Though he was fairly certain he'd feel better once he got back to Boston.

Mark had been kidding himself thinking that he could be a small-town boy. His Massachusetts roots ran too deep. He was used to the ball games, the Pops and the theater… All the things a big city could offer. If Ivy had been willing to be exposed to that, or at least meet him halfway, he might have thought of continuing their relationship. But she wouldn't even talk about it. Which ultimately proved how little she cared.

Mark didn't regret his time spent in Rosemont. But he wasn't eager to repeat it either. For all intents and purposes it had the earmarks of a heartbreak town. First, there'd been the disaster with Sandra. Then his unexpected entanglement with Ivy. He should have steered clear of hooking up with another woman when his heart was in a fragile state. He'd had impaired judgment. And just look where that judgment had landed him. Mark was grateful he'd hung on to his brownstone up north. He'd sleep better once he got home and put Rosemont behind him.

Chapter Eighteen

When Ivy got to the Coffee Connection on Monday, she was surprised that Walt wasn't waiting. Eustis arrived a few minutes later. "Morning!" she chirped, strapping on her apron.

"Where's Walt?"

Eustis's eyes danced with mirth. "Resting up, I'd imagine."

Ivy brought her hand to her mouth and giggled. "Eustis! You didn't?"

"It's none of your beeswax what I did or *didn't*..." But she was grinning just the same. "So how's about that hunk of *yours*?" Eustis wondered. "All the tongues in town are wagging. About him *and* your major display on the dance floor."

Ivy's face warmed. "We got a little carried away."

"I'll say!" Eustis glanced toward the door, then, seeing no one was coming, said confidentially, "So, what? Are the two of you back together?"

Ivy pursed her lips, delaying an answer.

"Ivy?" Eustis asked softly.

She wasn't crying yet, but if she looked at Eustis, she just might start. "No."

Eustis's voice rose in surprise. "No? But I thought... We all saw..." She blinked, and met Ivy's gaze. "You mean it was for show? That was one heck of a performance!"

A tear escaped her, and Ivy ran a hand across her cheek. "It wasn't pretend. At least, not on my part."

Eustis studied her sympathetically, then asked, "And on his?"

"I don't know."

"Well, how did you leave things?"

"I didn't. He did."

"What?"

"He's gone, Eustis," Ivy told her. "Long gone. Mark returned to Boston yesterday."

Later that week, Mark and Wayne sat sharing a pitcher of beer at their favorite burger joint near Harvard Square. Wayne frowned and refilled Mark's mug.

"I wish you'd told me about this earlier," he said. "I would have been there for you. You know that."

"I know, man, and I appreciate it. I do."

Wayne swigged from his mug and set it down. "Ivy Green! Imagine that. And there I thought you were still nursing your wounds, trying to get over Sandra."

"I am over Sandra."

"Sure, now. But I was talking at the time."

"I felt kicked around a little, sure. Until I thought it through."

"Well, I'm glad you got your head together on that one. Sandra was never my first pick for you."

"Why didn't you say so?"

Wayne shot him a smirk. "Who do you think told you to run?"

"Oh yeah, forgot that part."

They clinked mugs.

"Here's to new starts," Mark said.

"It's good to see you keeping it in perspective."

"I am. And part of my new view," he said, meeting his friend's eyes, "involves the bigger picture."

"What's that mean?"

"I've thought a lot about it, Wayne, and I'm tired. Exhausted from running from town to town. And you know what? I don't have to do it anymore. I've got lots of good people who can run those startups for me."

"And plenty of money to pay them," Wayne agreed. "So, what do you plan to do? Maintain your center of operations here?"

"I'll keep corporate in Boston, but I'm not sure I want to be a daily part of it."

"You're kidding, right?"

"Nope. I'm serious. I'm thinking of getting away to someplace different. Somewhere a little more laid-back. Then coming to Boston as needed."

"I can dig that point of view. Where do you have in mind?"

"No place yet, but I do know I need to get away. And soon."

"You're talking a vacation now?"

"A little R&R, yeah. I asked Janet to look into it and find me someplace special." Janet was Mark's top assistant and an absolute genie at pulling anything Mark desired out of the bottle.

"What kind of special?" Wayne wanted to know.

"Peaceful little getaway. Small-town atmosphere. Some place with a swimming hole."

"*Swimming hole?* What century is this?"

"With a nice little rope swing," Mark continued, his voice sounding dreamy. "The sort you ride right out over the water…"

"Are you nuts, man?"

"Don't knock it until you've tried it."

"Look, I know Janet is good, but I'm not sure she's *that* good."

"She's already found it."

"What?"

"Leaving at the end of next week."

"Hang on," Wayne said, a thought occurring. "You're not going back to Rosemont?"

"Buddy," Mark said with a grin, "far from it."

Ivy left the meeting feeling conflicted. Mark had been right about the people from DelaStar Drafts. They were super nice and would be really easy to work with. Plus, the group all seemed to have common goals in mind. She couldn't help but be excited by the projects they'd discussed, and was thrilled by the confidence the group placed in her abilities. All the locals vouched for her, and the DelaStar folks said Mark had spoken highly of her as well. That compliment felt like a double-edged sword, though, since it only reminded Ivy of Mark and the terrible way their relationship had ended. That was, if one could even consider what they'd had a relationship.

The truth was, Ivy didn't know how to categorize her former friendship with Mark. She only knew she was sad it was over. Mark had been gone nearly three weeks now, and she missed him badly. The prospect that it would be months before he returned made his absence pain her even more. His colleagues had said he was out of the country and indisposed, whatever that meant.

Though Ivy wasn't sure why she should look forward to his return to Rosemont anyway. It wasn't like he'd given any indication he'd want to see her. When he came back, it would be to tend to business matters, pure and simple. Ivy had heard he'd kept the cottage and was paying a company to clean it and maintain the lawn. Then again, since he'd probably rented it for the year, that made sense. Could be he planned to use it during occasional trips back to town.

Ivy shifted the folder in her hands as she walked toward her car. The DelaStar people had given her and the other Rosemont representatives paperwork to go through, including a prospectus. If things panned out, Ivy hoped to help oversee the fund and orchestrate the landscaping projects. The idea was for her to start slowly, with one major project, then gradually work her way into others. This would give her time to transition out of her job at the Coffee Connection while she and Eustis found and trained a replacement.

By all accounts, Ivy should be thrilled by this new opportunity. This was what she'd always wanted. More than she'd dreamed of. But the pit of her stomach felt sour, because the truth was this dream was being supplied by the one guy Ivy suddenly realized she wanted but knew she couldn't have: Mark Delacroix. Their backgrounds and lives couldn't have been more different, and neither one had appeared ready to budge. Ivy wasn't interested in joining his world any more than he was willing to commit to hers. At the time, Ivy had felt a sense of pride, as if she were standing her ground. Now, in the wee dark hours of so many mornings, she wondered if she'd made a mistake.

Mark was a wonderful man in so many ways. He was thoughtful and generous, with a kind, giving heart and two incredibly strong arms that could sweep her away. He'd listened to her about Austin, had supported her dreams and held her hand. And when he'd kissed her… Whoa. It was hard to erase the memory of that. Just like it was impossible to forget his gorgeous blue eyes and the way they'd sparkled in the sunlight that day at the swimming hole when he'd talked her into *letting go.* Now Ivy realized all she wanted to do was hold on. But it was too late.

Walt was still missing the next morning at the Coffee Connection.

"What did you do to him?" Ivy teased Eustis. "Put him in traction?"

"Shush!" she cried with a blush. "He's just busy this morning."

"Busy, hmm."

"Buying tickets, if you must know."

"Tickets! Eustis…" Ivy clutched her arm. "Spill."

Eustis shed a cheery glow. "Walt's taking me to Italy."

"*Italy?* For real?"

But from the look in Eustis's eyes there was no doubting it. "He asked me if there was anything I'd ever wanted to do but thought I couldn't."

"But *Italy*," Ivy said with a gasp. "Eustis, that's so sweet… And romantic."

Eustis's lips turned up in a dreamy smile. "Yeah, isn't it, though?"

"I guess he's still got it."

"Oh, he's got it all right." Eustis lowered her voice in a whisper. "And he's using it."

Ivy giggled and shielded their faces from a few morning patrons with a menu. "I can't believe you're really doing this. It seems so reckless and exciting."

"I know," Eustis said. "I'll be closing the shop for two weeks."

"This shop?"

"It's the only one I run," Eustis answered.

"When are you going?"

"The end of next month. I apply for my passport in the morning. Walt says we can rush it through."

Eustis's eyes lit up with an idea. "Say, maybe you should come with me?"

"To Italy?" Ivy asked in shock. "Wouldn't I be like a third—"

"Don't be silly, girl. I meant to the passport office."

"But why?"

"Because everyone should have one."

"Not me."

Eustis arched her eyebrows, which were plucked pencil-thin.

"You never know when adventure might call."

The next morning, Ivy stood at the line in the post office with Eustis. The place to apply for passports was in a small office in back. You had to fill out some forms, then ring a bell and wait. You also had to bring some ID and a birth certificate. Ivy felt foolish she'd let Eustis talk her into this. Where on earth was Ivy going to go?

"Stop being a killjoy," Eustis snapped, sitting beside her.

"What?"

"You're doubting yourself so loud I can hear it."

Eustis had said a passport was valuable for lots of things, including identification. If Ivy ever decided to move anywhere else and hoped to hold a job, she could show it as proof of citizenship. Not that Ivy had to do this for her work-study job in college. They'd accepted her driver's license and birth certificate just fine. Oh, and she might have had to show some utility bills.

Eustis rattled her paperwork in front of Ivy's face to get her attention. "Earth to Ivy."

"Why are you being so cranky today?"

"Because I hate seeing you down, when I'm happy," Eustis answered matter-of-factly."

"Who says I'm down?"

"Your face."

Ivy sighed and shook her head. Eustis was as loving as a mama bear, but sometimes she was as grouchy as one too. For some reason, she appeared to have her grump on today. "Shouldn't you be ecstatic?" she asked her. "Floating on air or something?"

"I am—about Walt. But now I'm starting to worry."

Ivy turned to her.

"About you, sweetie. I'm not sure if my running off to Italy's the right thing right now. Not with you still getting over—"

"Don't be ridiculous. I'm way over Austin."

"I wasn't going to say Austin, and you know it."

Ivy looked away, noting the lunchtime line was building. Fortunately, that was for folks mailing packages. Not many people applied for passports in Rosemont. Perhaps that was why this was taking so long.

"You know what I'm thinking," Eustis finally said. "I'm thinking you should call him."

"Mark? No! Why would I do that? He doesn't even want to hear from me."

"Who said so?"

"No one had to. If he'd wanted to talk to me, he would have phoned by now."

Eustis clucked her tongue and folded her arms across her chest. "Um-hm."

"What's that supposed to mean?"

"How do you know he's not thinking the same thing?"

Chapter Nineteen

Mark stared at the crystalline pond, deciding to forgo another jump. He'd dropped from that darned rope so many times already, he'd lost count of his attempts at *letting go.* He didn't know why it didn't seem to be working this time. The gesture had certainly done the trick in Rosemont. Then again, in Rosemont, he'd been shaking off a woman who wasn't right for him. Here, he was trying to forget about Ivy.

Mark surveyed the surrounding hills and the distant peaks of higher mountains. Janet had found a splendid spot. The cabin was quiet and isolated, and a good ten kilometers from the nearest town. Plus, it was in Canada.

Mark scooped his towel off the dock and headed back toward the cabin. It looked rustic but was outfitted with modern conveniences, including Wi-Fi. He'd been able to keep up with the office but in large part had gotten Boston to leave him alone. They understood he was on vacation and taking a much-needed break. Janet also vetted his communications so nobody bothered him unless absolutely necessary. He'd come up here for a couple of weeks but had decided to stay. He was really in no hurry to get back to Massachusetts. Besides, he still hadn't accomplished his number one vacation goal: putting thoughts of a pretty Southern belle out of his mind.

While he'd played it cool the evening of Austin's wedding, the truth was Ivy's words had stung him plenty. She was a true enigma in Mark's mind. Ivy was incredibly kind, thoughtful, and caring. He could tell that from her relationship with Eustis and how she cared about Rosemont. She was also smart and extra talented too. And yet, she had a stubborn streak about as long as a river was wide. He'd probably known only one other person as pigheaded. Mark hung his head at the admission. Himself.

What would it have hurt him to call her? Just once to see how she was doing, or even to ask how the Beautification Fund was coming along? He had that as a ready excuse, yet he hadn't used it. Mark had been a go-getter his entire life, and his success was a testament to that. But how successful was a man really, if he didn't surround himself with people he loved? Mark thought of his parents and the warm, loving relationship they shared. It hadn't always been perfect, and yeah, as a kid, he'd sometimes overheard them having words. But they'd always seemed to make up in spite of it. That's what commitment was, he supposed. Staying together in the hard times, not just the good.

If Ivy had given Mark any indication that she was interested, he would have pursued her. But her words came back to him across the miles. *"Then I'll wish you safe travels."* She hadn't pleaded with him to stay. On the contrary, she'd appeared glad to have him go. If not glad, at the very least relieved. And he'd been relieved to get away. Get away from another potential heartache. Mark frowned hard, understanding he hadn't succeeded. If possible, he felt worse about things now than he had before. So much for time healing all wounds, Mark thought with a grumble, pushing his way into the house.

Mark headed to the kitchen for a beer, his gaze falling on his cell phone. It sat on the wooden bar with the chair-style stools that divided the kitchen from the living area. He could call her now, he reasoned. Call her and say… Mark ran a hand through his hair, realizing how ridiculous that was. Call Ivy? Right. Totally out of the blue, and just to say what? *I've been thinking about you, you impossibly maddening woman—and can't get you out of my mind?* No. That probably wouldn't go over well. He'd have to rephrase that. Maybe add in a sweetener or two. Mark heaved a sigh and nabbed a brewski from the fridge, wondering who on earth he was fooling. Then, the next second, his phone rang.

Ivy clutched her cell with trembling fingers. She'd never done anything like this before. In the South, they called it eating crow. For all she knew, they called it that in Boston too. But the more she'd thought about it, the more she knew Eustis was right. Ivy wasn't sure what the outcome would be, but she'd decided she had to chance it. What if—by some slim miracle—Eustis was right? What if Mark *had* been thinking about her too? Then again, what if he'd moved on already and had another girlfriend? That was a possibility Ivy had to face. It had been two months since Mark left Rosemont, and what she and he had shared had hardly qualified as a full-blown relationship. Ivy's palm felt slick, and she was starting to lose her nerve. After the third ring, she was about to hang up. Then he answered.

"Ivy?" he asked in surprise.

She drew a breath, guessing she was still in his list of contacts and that was how he'd recognized her number. At least he hadn't erased her completely. "Hi," she began, shutting her eyes. "I know this is awkward."

"I can't believe you called," he rushed in. "I was just thinking about you."

"What?" She paused a moment to absorb this, opening her eyes.

His voice was low and gravelly. "In fact, I was about to call you."

Ivy's heart pounded. "You were?"

"The only thing was…" Ivy gripped her phone so hard her knuckles hurt. "I didn't think you'd answer."

Ivy let out a breath. "I definitely would have."

"You would have?"

"Yeah."

"Then, I'm sorry."

"About what?"

Mark paused a beat, and she could almost envision him pursing his lips. "That I didn't call before."

"Mark, I… I don't really know how to begin."

"Just say it."

"I wanted to apologize—for how everything ended. For maybe giving you the wrong impression."

"I might have given you the wrong impression too." His tone was tinged with remorse.

"How?"

"By acting like I didn't want to see you again."

For the first time in two months, hope bloomed in her heart. "Do you?"

"I do, if you'll have me."

"I was calling to ask you the same thing."

"To ask about getting together, you mean?"

"Yeah."

"In Rosemont?"

"No, in Boston."

"Boston?" he asked with surprise.

"I've been doing a lot of thinking about how unyielding I was. I mean, you've seen my world.

There's no reason I can't catch a glimpse of yours.
Take in a ball game, tour a famous university or two."

Mark laughed warmly, unable to believe this was
happening. It was like a dream come true. His dream.
"I'd *love* for you to come to Boston. I'd have a blast
showing you around."

"There are no swimming holes there, I'll bet."

Mark stared out the window at his private pond, a
thought occurring. "Nope, but I've got one here."

"Where are you exactly?"

"Canada."

"*Canada?*"

"Yeah." His lips parted in a grin. "Want to come
and visit?"

"To Canada? Like out of the country?"

"We have a thing or two to talk over, don't you
think? Some lost ground to cover?"

"But in Canada?" she repeated again, like she
couldn't believe it.

"I can have Janet buy your ticket."

"Who's Janet?"

"My assistant in Boston." Mark's wheels processed
the whole thing quickly. Ivy was coming to Canada! He
couldn't wait to take her in his arms and tell her all
those things he'd wanted to say. Then his more
practical side kicked in. "You do have a passport?"

"Just applied for one this morning. With Eustis!"

"What?"

"Walt's taking her to Italy."

"No kidding?" Mark grinned to think he'd had a
hand in that. "That's sweet."

"Yes, and very romantic."

Mark could think up all sorts of ways to get romantic with Ivy in this place. It was cozy and quaint, and the temperatures dropped enough at night to light a fire in the stone hearth. "Well, that's good. Good you've applied for your passport. I'll have Janet run down your paperwork and see if she can expedite it."

"What does that mean?"

"That means I'm going to work on getting you to Canada, sweetheart. Just as soon as humanly possible. Tell me that you'll come."

Ivy dropped her voice an octave, accentuating her acceptance. "*Oh, yeah.*"

Three weeks later, Ivy got out of the car that had carried her from the airport. The cabin was adorable and set at the edge of a forest with a broad clearing in back. She spied the glimmer of water beyond it and hoped it was swimmable. Ivy couldn't believe she was really here! In Canada! Another country! She'd never even been out of her state.

Mark emerged from the building looking stunning in jeans and a casual shirt. She'd nearly forgotten how good-looking he was, his rugged face offsetting his buff frame. The driver pulled away, and Mark took her in his arms hoisting her off the ground in a bear hug. "You made it!"

She hugged him back, kicking her feet in the air and laughing with delight. "Yes! All the way to Canada!"

For these past three weeks, they'd talked on the phone every day. Sometimes more than once per day. She'd admitted to Mark she'd never been much beyond Rosemont, except to her college town that was a few hours away.

He set her down to gaze at her, his blue eyes sparkling in the sunlight.

"You're a world traveler now."

"I know," she said with a giggle, "and I like it." What was not to like about the business-class ticket Janet had supplied, and the extra perks along the way, like having a prearranged car meet her at the airport?

"The flight went well?"

"It was perfect."

He leaned his forehead against hers and grinned. "I'm glad."

"So, this is where you've been all this time." She nodded toward the cabin. "Your secret hideaway?"

"It's *our* hideaway now," he said with a wink. "Come on, let me show you around!"

He took her bags and carried them inside, while Ivy practically floated behind him. She still couldn't believe this was happening. That she was here with Mark. That he *wanted* her here.

After a short tour of the house, he led her out back, where Ivy absorbed the view. "It's gorgeous."

"I thought it was great before," he said, taking her hand. "I like it even better now."

He smiled as her gaze traveled over the pond.

"A rope swing!" she proclaimed, pleased. "I can't believe it."

"I thought it was for letting go, but now I get that it's for something else."

She looked up at him, and he squeezed her hand.

"I think it's meant for learning to hold on— together."

"Could be dangerous," she teased. "Sooner or later, we'll both be in for a fall."

He spun her and took her in his arms. "Oh yeah?"

Ivy's pulse fluttered wildly. "Yeah."

"In that case, we'd better practice up."

Then, he brought his lips to hers in a kiss.

Epilogue

Nine months later, Mark found himself in a tuxedo outside the chancel of Rosemont Holy Trinity Church. "Not planning on running this time?" Wayne ribbed from nearby.

Mark met his buddy's eyes and grinned. "Not on your life."

"I'm glad to see you happy," Wayne said. "Looks like you finally got this right."

Mark peeked through the door into the cram-packed church. All of Rosemont had turned out, and every single person was pulling for him and Ivy. Including Austin and Caroline, who were well on their way to having their first baby by now.

Eustis and Walt said they would have procreated if they could have, but they were way past that. Both had surprised the whole town by eloping in Italy and had been living together in wedded bliss ever since. Ivy's work with the Rosemont Beatification Fund had been so successful, Mark had suggested she travel with him to help get similar initiatives started in other locales. After a year of doing that, they planned to settle in Rosemont, because both had agreed it was an ideal place to raise a family.

Mark would still keep his brownstone in Boston to use when he traveled there on business, and Ivy would accompany him whenever possible. But their most important piece of real estate was a sweet little cabin in the Canadian woods that would always hold a special place in both of their hearts. They hoped to take their kids there some day, spending lazy summer afternoons instructing the little ones on the merits of a rope swing.

"It's time," Wayne told him, patting his shoulder.

Mark followed Wayne through the door and into the sanctuary, where music played. Thankfully, it wasn't "Ave Maria." Both he and Ivy had agreed on that. Soon the bridesmaids arrived, including Grace and Eustis. Then before long, Ivy appeared in the doorway. Mark caught his breath on her beauty because she looked like an angel. She was even more stunning in white than he'd envisioned all that time ago at Austin's wedding. Then again, all that time ago, he'd never imagined he'd be so lucky. He never could have guessed that—one day—Ivy would be his.

She met him at the altar and smiled, her cheeks aglow. Brown eyes shone with deep affection, the kind that Mark knew would last forever—in good times and in bad.

"I love you," he whispered taking her hand.

"I love you back."

Then they said their vows and pledged that neither would leave the other—ever again.

The End

A Note from the Author

Thanks for reading *The Getaway Groom.* I hope you enjoyed it. If you did, please help other people find this book.

1. This book is lendable, so lend it to a friend who you think might like it so that she (or he) can discover me, too.

2. Help other people find this book: write a review.

3. Sign up for my newsletter so you can learn about the next book as soon as it's available. Write to GinnyBairdRomance@gmail.com with "newsletter" in the subject heading.

4. Come like my Facebook page: https://www.facebook.com/GinnyBairdRomance.

5. Connect with me on Twitter: https://twitter.com/GinnyBaird.

6. Visit my website: http://www.ginnybairdromance.com for details on other books available at multiple outlets now.